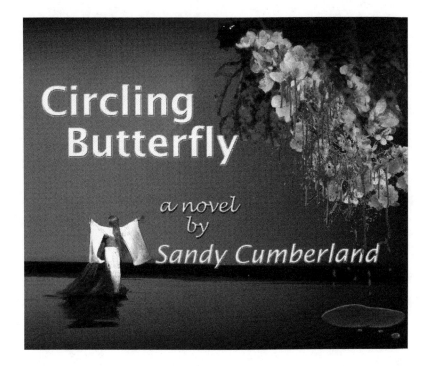

This is a work of fiction. Although the author has strived to maintain historical accuracy, the story is also based around another work of fiction, the opera *Madama Butterfly,* by Giacomo Puccini, with an Italian libretto by Luigi Illica and Giuseppe Giacosa, and the stories herein are products of the author's imagination.

Circling Butterfly Copyright © 2019 Sandy Cumberland
All rights reserved.
ISBN-13: 978-1-9992290-0-9

Jacket Art by R.H.M.

circlingbutterfly.com

For my amazing kids, Kate & Will, whose wisdom, compassion, humor & love are the cornerstones of my life

Acknowledgments

Madama Butterfly. The heartbreaking tale of love and loss. Even the non-opera-goers amongst us can name that one, and, if pushed, can probably come up with a close approximation of the story. A young geisha in turn-of-the-century Japan falls in love and marries an American Naval officer. She knows the marriage is arranged, but thinks their love is genuine, so when he returns to America she waits for him. Three years later, he returns, but with his beautiful American wife in tow. Butterfly discloses that they have a son together. He and his wife offer to take the boy back to America. Butterfly kills herself. End of story.

I remember my first "Madama Butterfly". I mean, I already knew the music and the story. My mother, who struggled with hearing loss, rarely played music in the house, but when she did, as often as not, it would be an opera. I was thirteen years old, attending the opera as a part of a student performance by the Canadian Opera Company, at the old O'Keefe Centre in Toronto. Sitting in the nosebleed section, surrounded by my classmates, none of whom had any interest in the show, but were awfully happy to have an afternoon out of school. When the house lights dimmed, I fell instantly into the story. By the time Pinkerton cried out the iconic "Butterfly" as she lay dying at centre stage, I was sobbing uncontrollably. Hooked. Completely hooked.

I saw a couple more productions through my teen years. Each one had the same devastating effect on me. I can't say it was Butterfly in particular, or opera in general, that lead to my career as a stage manager. That honour falls to the world of ballet. But it came as no surprise that ten years after graduating from the University of Ottawa with a BA in Theatre, I found myself as the stage manager of Pacific Opera Victoria in Victoria, BC. And within the year, I was working on the first of several "Madama Butterfly"s with that company. I have to say, it never got easier to call the final lighting cues and the main curtain in, through the nightly tears.

Needless to say, this one is probably my favourite of the "Top Ten" operas - the standard repertoire that most companies draw on for at least one of the shows in their season to keep the subscribers happy. Sure, it has flaws. And, sure, in this modern day, some of the themes can be construed as painfully sexist, even misogynistic. But the haunting music by Puccini, Butterfly's heart-wrenching overnight vigil waiting for her man to arrive, only to be shattered by his betrayal, and those final moments...

But... But... What about the stories around Butterfly. What about her faithful maid, Suzuki? Sharpless, the US consul who befriends the husband? And what becomes of Butterfly's little boy that she prophetically called Sorrow? We meet them all in the opera, but only as fleeting glimpses. What of their lives? What of their pain?

It's the triptych of these three stories that are told here. The lives that surrounded, loved, and mourned the delicate Butterfly. The stories of Suzuki, Sharpless and Thomas. Knowing the depth and breadth of their lives and their relationships with our heroine and each other brings fullness to Butterfly's life as well, and makes her story all the more tragic.

I make no claims to be an historian. I take refuge in the knowledge that I am basing these stories, not on the historical accuracy of turn-of-the-twentieth-century Japan, but on an opera, written by an Italian, about a Japanese woman and an American man. I have sought to create a world for my characters that closely approximates their lives as they would have been, but in the end it is a world entirely emerging from my imagination.

There are many wonderful people who have supported and nurtured me as I wrote this book: my children Kate Camenzind and Will Halliday and their father Bruce Halliday who always cheered me on; my sister Chris Cumberland and her husband Sam Hauserman who fed me and picked me up whenever I fell down. I thank Connie McConnell for loving my dog Pequena as much as I do, my oldest-and-dearest, Carolyn Trickey-Bapty, for always believing, Barbara Bell of the Kingston WritersFest for bravely offering to read and critique my first draft, Melanie Froh Teichroeb, my Shield Maiden for giving it a Viking warrior read-through, R.H.M., and many, many friends who have been so supportive. I thank Alice Bacon and John Carswell and their amazing shop, the Brentwood Bay Village Empourium, where I set up my "office," a place to work for hours at a time over a single Americano.

Circling Butterfly

Suzuki

Suzuki

It was the stench. The putrid combination of congealing blood, shit and panic. And the sound. The squawk followed by "Thwack".

Then running, out the door, grabbing our filthy basket on the way, my sister and I circled the house and followed the stream to the point where the willow signalled the bend. We knew as we passed the willow to suck in a deep breath and try to hold it as long as possible. Even so, the disgusting smell found its way into our noses and onto our skin.

The deep red puddle glistened around the stump from the most recent kill. All the women in our village used this spot so the stench stayed clear of their homes. Only the poorest families, like ours, lived downwind of the stump.

But Mama was clever and turned this to her advantage. Once the neighbour had taken her decapitated chicken home to prepare it for dinner, Katsumi and I sprang into action. Our job was to get there before the wind stole all the stray feathers. We gathered them up in our basket.

You had to be very careful with your footing though. One time I was trying to reach a nice big feather stuck by congealed blood to the stump. I didn't want to step in the dark brown mud so I stretched out as far as I could. Next thing I knew, my hands slapped down into the goo, dying them bright red. I watched in horror as the ring of pink formed around the hems of my sleeves. I felt droplets of slime dripping down my cheeks.

"Katsumi!" I yelled. "I'm stuck! Don't let me fall right in!"

My sister was able to pull me back to my feet by pulling on my obi. It was cold that day and the stream was icy, but I waded in and scrubbed my hands and face raw. That kimono with the stained sleeves taunted me for an entire year until I finally outgrew it.

Once we had all the feathers gathered, we took them home. There was a corner behind the house, beside a little plum tree, that got lots of sunshine and very little wind. There we laid out an old cloth. Katsumi squatted and took each feather from the basket, one at a time. Each one was carefully inspected, then, with a damp rag, she cleaned off any residual blood or dirt. The little feathers from around the chicken's bum were the finest because they were soft and downy, but they took the most cleaning to get the shit off. And, oh, did they stink! Once she was satisfied with a feather, she carefully handed it to me to place on the cloth in the sunshine. My responsibility was to ensure that they didn't blow away and to run chasing any that escaped.

After the feathers had dried sufficiently, we gathered them up in a clean basket and took it inside next to the spot Mama did her sewing. At night, lying on my mat, I listened to my parents softly talking in the dim lantern light as Mama sewed scraps of fabric into cushion covers, which she would then stuff with the chicken feathers. Papa sold them in his tailor shop. The cushions didn't bring in much money but, since most of the homes in our village had dirt floors, or maybe wood on dirt, the cushions were generally appreciated.

I couldn't have been older than seven or eight when my parents sold me. We lived in rooms at the back of Papa's parents' home in a village on the sea. I never did know the name of either the village or the sea. Either my mother was very fertile or my parents could not resist the act of procreating - though now that I think of it, I cannot imagine where or when they might have committed those intimate acts in our tiny home overrun with children - but life became harder and harder as they produced more and more mouths to feed and little bodies to clothe. My father worked two jobs. Before dawn he would be down at the docks helping the fishermen prepare their nets. Then, when the boats had all been loosed to catch the morning's breeze, he would climb the path to his tiny shop in the village where he sat at the open doorway hunched over needle and thread, sewing simple but beautiful obis for the young women of the village. My mother had her hands full at home, cooking and cleaning for her in-laws in exchange for our free rooms, and caring for her growing brood, usually with one baby on her back, which balanced nicely the one growing in her belly. My two older brothers, as soon as they were able, went to the docks with their father to offer their help for the few coins tossed their way, then to collect a basket of seaweed to take home. My oldest sister helped care for the youngest, bathing and feeding and dressing.

I do wish I could remember my brothers' and sisters' names…

One morning I awoke to hear my parents' whispered tones in the next room. I felt the air rustle as the curtain moved and then Papa was kneeling next to the mat my sister and I shared. He reached over me and gently stroked my sister's hair, then saw in the half-light that I was staring up at him.

"Good morning Papa-san. Is something wrong?" I asked.

He paused for a moment then brushed his fingertips across my forehead whispering "Be well, Suzuki". Then he silently rose, pushed past the curtain again, and moments later I heard his footsteps crunching on the path.

I must have fallen back asleep, because when I opened my eyes again a soft light filtered into the room. The curtain was pushed aside. My oldest sister was swaddling the baby and I could see my mother through the doorway, dressed in her one decent kimono that still fit over her swollen belly, folding clothes and trinkets into two baskets. Once we had dressed, Mama-san looked at my ten-year-old sister and me expectantly from the doorway. The oldest sister, holding the baby and ably fingering rice into the mouths of two toddlers, smiled wanly at Katsumi and me and nodded at the two baskets.

My mother set a brisk pace down the path to the village. This must be mending to go to Papa, I thought. But then we turned away from Papa's shop. Perhaps she is hoping to trade these items for a fish at the docks? But no, we marched straight past the docks and started up the hill out of the village. Without a single word spoken we continued to walk. Along the coast, past the next village, then the next, well past anywhere I had ever seen before. When the sun began to lower in the sky, Mama-san stopped at a rough little inn. The sun-bleached thatched roof was thread-bare in spots, the two windows facing the road were covered with dusty, splintered boards, and a tattered curtain decorated with faint cherry blossoms and mud splatters was still in the heavy twilight air. She led us into the dark room where I heard her whisper to the innkeeper's wife and hand her a few coins. The woman looked pityingly at my sister and me, our heads drooped with exhaustion, our hands barely holding our baskets of precious cargo. She led us to a little table and placed three cups of tea before us, then three small bowls of rice with a sprinkling of chopped dried seaweed on top. Katsumi and I gratefully dropped our baskets and flopped down on the scratchy tatami mat, starving and thirsty but barely able to keep our eyes open to eat. Mama-san sipped her tea, standing over us, staring ahead at nothing.

That night we slept on a single mat laid out in a corner of the cooking room. Despite the heat and humidity, my sister and I pressed our warm bodies to either side of Mama-san the way I imagined baby monkeys would cling to their mother. Both our arms draped over her belly, protected and protecting. We still had no idea where Mama-san was taking us but knew that silence and obedience was being demanded of us. Any time I thought to question her, I would remember the sad look in Papa-san's eyes and would stay quiet. But none of this made any sense. Thinking

SureFit 2B sport locks are compatible with SureFit 2C receivers and are available for three receiver power levels: LP, MP and HP.

The sport lock tail and the receiver tube should be going in opposite directions.

Correct!

The sport lock is flush with the receiver body and the entire nozzle is visible.

Incorrect!

The sport lock is not pushed back completely flush with the receiver body; a portion of the nozzle is covered by the sport lock. **In this case the dome will not attach properly!**

For assistance, contact ReSound Technical Support

Manufacturer according to FDA:
GN ReSound North America
8001 E Bloomington Freeway
Bloomington, MN 55420
USA
1-800-248-4327
pro.resound.com

Manufacturer according to Health Canada:
GN Hearing A/S
Lautrupbjerg 7
DK-2750 Ballerup
Denmark
pro.resound.com

Distributor in Canada:
ReSound Canada
2 East Beaver Creek Road, Building 3
Richmond Hill, ON L4B 2N3
Canada
1-888-737-6863
pro.resound.com

401635000 Rev B 2021.03

Receiver Replacement Notification

The receiver on your hearing aid was replaced during service. The new SureFit 2C receivers require the use of SureFit 3 domes and have the same acoustic performance as SureFit 2B receivers*.

SureFit 2C (single ring)

SureFit 2B (double ring)

SureFit 3 domes are a light grey with a blueish hue to them and are available in open, closed, tulip and power domes.

*It is recommended to utilize the same receiver type (SureFit 2B or SureFit 2C) on both hearing instruments in a binaural fitting.

back, I could remember hearing what sounded like whispered arguments late in the night. And sometimes I would catch a look of sorrow in Mama-san's eye before she would quickly return to her chores. If our mother had done something wrong, and our father was exiling her, why would she not have taken all the children? Especially the baby! I longed to talk it all through with Katsumi but the steady breathing coming from the other side of the mat testified to the exhausted sleep she had succumbed to.

Just at that moment, Mama-san's body adjusted and she raised her hand to my face. Her surprisingly cool fingers stroked my brow, just like she did when I was an infant and restless in my bed. Over and over those fingers brushed, gently forcing my eyes to close each time until they grew too heavy to stay open.

"Hush, my little Suzuki. We have a long journey ahead of us still. Rest your eyes. Rest your mind. All will be well, you will see," she whispered.

I am kneeling at a shrine. I am in a beautiful house but there is strange, over-sized furniture all around me, as if I have entered a giant's home. I am chanting, but I am also crying. Far away I can hear men moaning as if in dreadful pain, and a child weeping. Suddenly a wind whips up and cherry blossoms begin to fall. I raise my eyes to them as they drop silently all around me. For some reason it is not at all strange that the blossoms are falling inside the house. One blossom falls on my uplifted cheek and I feel moisture where it landed. I wipe my cheek and when I look at my hand it has a red smear on it. I look around the floor and the furniture - all the blossoms seem to melt when they land, leaving a bright red puddle. Odd, I think. The blossoms fall heavier. I try to return to my chanting but I can see from the corners of my eyes that the puddles are expanding to meet each other. Where blossoms have landed on the huge tables and chairs, the red liquid is flowing over the edges to join the pools forming on the floor. The reality suddenly hits me that this liquid is, in fact, blood! I stand up, my tatami mat creating a small island in what has become a sea of blood. I raise my kimono slightly and try to step through the redness, but it is too slippery and I am very afraid to fall. I cry out for help, but I know the keening men and the crying child are too far away.

My mother's arm tucked under me and pulled me closer to her, cooing softly. I wrapped my arm tightly over her belly and gratefully slipped back into a peaceful sleep.

The next morning, the innkeeper glowered at us as we quickly gathered up our things. His wife gave us each a little cup of tea and handed Mama-san a spoonful of sticky rice, wrapped in a ragged grey cloth. We bowed and bowed as we backed to the door and out into the cool morning air. All three of us stopped, took a deep breath, rearranged our baskets on our arms, and Mama-san turned us down the road, once again heading farther away from home.

For two more days we traveled like this, walking all day, stopping along the way only for tea and a bowl of rice, or a tiny piece of fish from a boat in a harbour. The first day we must have been near a temple or shrine, for we seemed to be constantly stepping off the path to bow as a group of priests or monks walked past. Near the end of the day, as we paused once again, I glanced up as the men were passing. An ancient priest caught my eye! I tried to look down as I had been taught to do, but he held my eye with a firm look. Then a twinkling appeared in his eye, a broad smile lit up his face and he stopped and came to where we stood.

"Okaasan," he said to my mother, "your little ones look ready to sleep where they stand. Have you a long journey?"

With her head still lowered, my mother whispered "Dai-osho-sama, we are only on a three day journey, from Kumamoto to Nagasaki. It is not too far."

"Well, perhaps the little girls are hungry?"

"Thank you Dai-osho-sama, but we will eat when we rest tonight."

"But Mama-san, I am hungry now!" I blurted before I could stop the words from escaping. My mother's hand gripped mine so tightly I almost cried out. The anger in her eyes made me immediately flush bright pink and lower my head in shame.

"Of course you are, child. Walking is hard work not to be done on an empty stomach." With those words he reached into the deep, wide sleeve of his robe and, like a magician, pulled out a little packet of rice, beautifully wrapped in seaweed.

"My novice is a very bright young man and he knows me well. He always collects a little rice from the kitchen in the morning for me to snack on around mid-day. Today I did not feel I needed to eat it. I must have been saving it for you." And he held out the little bundle to my mother.

She looked up at him, her eyes full of both shame and gratitude, and received his gift, for it would have been an insult not to. The priest then stepped in front of my sister and placed her hand on her head in blessing.

"This child is kind and loving. She will marry well one day and bear many children," he said, smiling at our mother, "much like her Okaasan."

He then stepped to me. Instead of resting his hand on my head, he slowly and carefully lowered himself to crouch face-to-face with me.

"You, child, what is your name?"

I looked up quickly at my mother, who simply nodded at me to answer the man.

"Suzuki, sir. My name is Suzuki."

"And how old are you, Suzuki-san?"

It took me a moment to remember. "Eight years old. Um, I think... Sir."

"Well, Suzuki-san, you are smart and strong-willed. Most of all, though, you are loyal and brave. Whomever you come to serve will be honoured to have you at their side. I hope our paths cross again one day." He then reached into his magic sleeve again and pulled out two small coins. He pressed one into my hand, then cautiously raised himself back up to stand over us. He took Katsumi's hand and rested the second coin there, then stepped back and gave us a small bow before moving on to join the other priests on the path. We both stood silently, bent deep in a bow of gratitude. Tears burnt the corners of my eyes.

That night we slept as well as we could, on a small mat Mama-san had carried on her back, under a ficus tree. She drew some water from a nearby stream, and we once again thanked the priest as we shared the packet of rice and seaweed. Katsumi even snatched a persimmon from a low hanging branch and snuck it back to us in her sleeve. When she produced the fruit from her sleeve, she presented it in a perfect imitation of the priest and the three of us found ourselves laughing for the first time in days. We were hungry, tired and dusty from our travels, but that was a wonderful day!

Mama-san had told the priest that we were only travelling for three days. Katsumi and I still had no idea where this journey would take us. She and I had stolen a few moments alone here and there to confer and share what we knew and to realize that we really knew nothing at all.

It was still dark when I awoke. Through the branches of the ficus I could just make out a thin line of morning on the horizon. We had placed ourselves well away from the path, but even so I could hear the sound of a mule braying, and a man's angry voice. The sounds did not pass out of hearing range as I had expected if the driver was urging his beast along the path.

Finally, curiosity got the better of me, and I slipped away from Mama-san's protective sleeping arm. I snuck down to investigate. In the dim light I could see a man standing, stick in hand, bent over a large mass lying on the road. As my eyes adjusted in the dim light, I could make out the form of a mule, down on its side, braying piteously. One pannier lay heavy on his side, filled with rocks. The second must have been painfully under him. Several rocks scattered the path, having slipped from the over-full panniers when he dropped from exhaustion. I could see the top bag rise and fall as the beast struggled to breathe. The white of his eye glinted in the faint morning light and I could see steam puff from his flared nostrils with each desperate breath.

Over him, the man continued to yell, berating the mule to stand up, whipping him with the stick over and over. Even in the semi-darkness, I could see the welts forming, and the scars on the poor creature's haunch from a lifetime of beatings.

I stood in the shadow, breathless, willing the man to stop. After what seemed like an eternity he finally through the stick to the side in frustration. The mule's braying had softened to the sound of a baby's whimper. The man walked around the mule, surveying the rocks strewn on the road. He calmly bent over and picked up one large one and juggled it around in his hands until a sharp angle pointed away from him. He moved to the mule's head and the beast tried in vain to raise his head to him. Without hesitation the man smashed the rock between the eyes of the mule. I watched in horror as he struck again and again. The face split open and blood began to pour out onto the ground. The mule thrashed its legs at first, desperately trying to get up and escape, but he was pinned down by the rocks and his own exhaustion. On the third blow the legs fell still. Over and over the rock pounded the mule's face into an unrecognizable pulp. Blood had pooled around him, and ran over the dry, dusty path toward me.

I watched in horror. I realized I had forced my fist into my mouth to prevent me from crying out loud. I dropped to my knees and said a silent prayer that the beast had been released from his suffering and hoped that the gods would grant him a better life when he returned.

The man, his anger finally spent, dropped the rock and pulled out a rag. He calmly wiped the blood spatters from his hands and face and repocketed the rag. Then he started collecting his rocks and piling them at the side of the road, careful to avoid the blood. Against my will, I glanced once more at the battered remains of the mule's face. Flies feasted on the tattered flesh.

While the man was still occupied, I slipped back, deeper into the shadows, back to the ficus tree. I had just lay down on the sleeping mat as Mama-san stirred. She turned to me with a smile "Did you manage to sleep all right on this hard ground?"

"Yes, Mama-san," I smiled back, pretending to wipe sleep, and not tears, from my eyes. "I feel quite rested."

"Good, for today will be a very important day for you and your sister."

She led us to the little stream and we bathed as best we could. She then sat us down and, one at a time, she meticulously brushed and pinned up our hair. I could feel her hard belly press against my back as she worked to control my long thick hair. When she was done, she stood back and appraised us thoroughly, then reached in to the bottom of her basket. She pulled out two hair ornaments. Fragile, delicate cascades of white petals fell from matching ornate silver combs.

"Your grandmother, my mother, gave me these when I was a young woman," she said, with a touch of melancholy in her voice. "I think they will be just right for you two today." And she slid the combs into our hair so the flowers spilled almost to our shoulders.

Without another word, we gathered our things and headed for the road. I was grateful that, by having gone to the stream, we would descend farther along than where we had slept, so I wouldn't be forced to revisit the dead mule and all that blood.

By the time the sun was at its peak, we were being jostled and bumped by many people and carts on the road. There were homes and shops very close together. The crowds and the noise were overwhelming. We were approaching a busy port and Katsumi and I tucked close in behind Mama-san. Her head held high, she looked like one of the huge steamships I could see anchored in the harbour, cutting through the crowds like waves.

Just when I thought I would expire from thirst, Mama-san stopped outside a dingy little fish market. Dozens of fish hung from hooks in the ceiling, with many more piled in heaps on tables outside. Past the hanging fish there seemed only darkness. She signalled us to sit down on a stone bench outside, left her basket with us and went in. A few minutes later, she returned with little clay cups filled with cold water for each of us. The shopkeeper followed her out and pointed first down the road, then up the hill away from the harbour. We gratefully drank the water, bowed many times in thanks to the shopkeeper and went off in the direction he had pointed.

A short distance up the hill, Mama-san stopped abruptly in front of the biggest house I had ever seen. It had two storeys, a welcoming front porch that overlooked a koi pond with a little bridge to cross from the road. She looked me over, made a perfunctory effort to tame my hair, then led us to the front door.

A young girl answered the door immediately. She wore an elegant kimono with several ornate hair ornaments and had red paint on her eyebrows and lower lip. My mouth must have dropped open! I looked from the girl, to my mother, to my sister, then back to the girl. She looked to be about fourteen or fifteen and said nothing, just stood with her eyes downcast, waiting.

"We are here to see Junko-san. Please tell her Suzuki is here." With the sound of my name, I surfaced from my initial shock and looked at Mama-san, but she kept her eyes fixed on the young woman. We were led into an entryway. Beyond I could see a room with a tatami floor and several cushions arranged around a large teak table. There were other rooms as well, but each of those were hidden behind beautifully painted screens.

After a few minutes an older woman appeared from around one of the screens. Behind her I caught a glimpse of a huge wooden desk, covered with neat stacks of paper. The room was dark and windowless, with only a lamp at one corner of the desk to illuminate the space.

The woman exclaimed, "Mariko-san," as she rushed to my mother. They joined hands and looked into each other's eyes.

"Hello Junko-san," said Mama-san. "It is so good to see you again."

"Let me look at you. Another one on the way, very soon, I see. And yet you don't seem to have aged since we were girls."

Junko put one hand on Mama-san's belly, while Mama-san self-consciously reached up to pat her hair. Like mine, Mama-san's thick hair did not tend to stay where it belonged. They both smiled, then Junko led us into the bright open room.

She glanced at my sister briefly, then turned her gaze to me. Up close, I could see that her cream coloured kimono was finely embroidered with images of cranes and bamboo, all done in white thread so as to be almost invisible. Her hair was pulled up in a fashion I had never seen before, with one simple ornament of cream and orange flowers. Like the girl's, her eyebrows were painted red as were both her lips.

She looked me up and down and I found myself fidgeting under her eyes.

"Suzuki! Be still!" my mother admonished.

"It's all right, Mariko-san," said the woman. She spoke softly and I could see kindness in her eyes. "No one likes to be inspected."

The young girl brought tea with little cakes, as sweet and moist as spring water on a hot day. My mother and the beautiful woman chatted like old friends, exchanging stories of people they once knew and places I had never heard of before. I heard Mama laugh, a tinkling girlish laugh, that made her look and sound decades younger than the tired woman who had entered this house with my sister and me. All too soon, she looked at me and brushed invisible crumbs from her kimono as she rose. Katsumi and I rose to leave as well, but Mama caught my hand.

"No, Suzuki, you stay here. This is to be your home now. You listen to Junka-san and do what you are told. She is your oka-san."

"But Mama-san," I cried, looking from her to Katsumi in horror. "Mama-san! You're leaving me here?" Mama's eyes held mine in silence. "What about Katsumi? Can't she stay here with me? Mama-san, I don't want to be left here alone!"

Finally she spoke. "Katsumi must come with me. Junka-san has found her a wonderful house to live where she will be fortunate to learn the tea ceremony. One day she will serve noblemen, perhaps even the Emperor himself. Katsumi, we must leave now. There is a train shortly that will take you to Kyoto. Meiko-san will meet you when you arrive to take you to your new home." A single tear slipped from Mama's eye and glistened on her cheek. "You are good girls. Your father and I are both proud of you. You have been given great opportunities to have better lives." She bowed low to Junka, who gently took Mama's arms to raise her back up. They looked into each other's eyes for a long moment, then in an act both shockingly familiar and lovingly tender, Junka placed her tiny hands with their long manicured nails on either side of Mama's large belly. Mama smiled and gave a tiny shrug, then reached down to briefly touch the flowers of my hair ornament. Mama-san then nodded to Katsumi and left the room with my sister in her wake.

After a moment of silence, the young girl came in to collect the tea things. Junka stopped her and beckoned her to come to where we stood. I felt the woman's hand rest on my back.

"Suzuki. I promise it will be all right. I will teach you everything you need to know. For now all you need to know is that your job is to help and care for my young protégée here. One day she will be a fine geisha and you will be her servant. Suzuki, I would like you to meet Cio-Cio-san."

Junka was right. She did patiently teach me. I learned how to wrap Cio-Cio in her elaborate kimonos and how to dress her hair in the traditional hoko-shimada style, full of ornaments of flowers and butterflies. I was taught how to walk correctly, when to bow my head and lower my eyes. I spent days, weeks, learning how to kneel down with a full tray of tea and cups without tripping on my skirts or kicking off a shoe. Cio-Cio went off to dancing and singing lessons, and practiced her songs on the shamisan, plucking at the three strings until her fingers bled.

At night we shared a room. Lying side by side on our mats, we whispered stories of our childhoods. Cio-Cio reached across the moon-drenched floor for my hand and wove tales of our lives together, she as a meigi, the most sought-after geisha in the land, and me by her side, her faithful friend and servant. I knew then I would be loyal unto death and utterly in love.

Before we knew it, Cio-Cio was called upon to entertain Junka-san's guests in the evenings. I would painstakingly prepare her dress, her hair, her make-up. I would watch her pass through the shoji screens into the tea room. I would stand for hours in the shadows where I could hear her tinkling laughter rise and fall, spinning its web around the men's deep, loud voices. Then the men would sit silently in awe and Cio-Cio would pick up her shamisan to play and sing a sorrowful song of love and loss. Finally she would brighten their spirits again with a joyful, flirtatious dance. At the end of the dance, as the men applauded and noisily expressed their pleasure, in my mind's eye I could see her bow deeply to each one in turn, then the screens would silently slide open and she would back out of the room. Out of their world and back into mine. Into the night, as I removed the make-up and ornaments and unraveled her long silky hair, she would regale me with stories about the men. She would imitate the way they sat, the way they spoke, how uncouthly they slurped their tea, and we would laugh and laugh.

Months passed. Autumn turned to winter and soon the cherry blossoms began to peek out again. At night their sweet aroma would slip through the open window and coil itself mysteriously around my nostrils, and my dreams would be full of images of the bright pink boughs in buckets of water, neutralizing the fishy smell that rose up from the docks and tried to take over my father's shop. Once a week all through blossom season, my brother would cut the boughs and my oldest sister and I would carry them down to the shop to replace the wilted ones. Sometimes in my dreams the flowers were so wilted that they became nothing but a puddle of sticky pink with a rotting smell. I could hear Papa-san berating us to clean up the mess and go so he could get back to his work.

Night time. Our tatami mats separated by a rice paper shoji screen. Cio-Cio's mat and sleep pad were carefully laid out with soft cotton bedding and often with a fresh orchid blooming, or a delicate pine bonsai nearby, filling the air with their sweetness. My pad lay in a corner of the room. The screen allowed only the most diffuse moonlight and the slightest of breezes to pass from the window.

I understood my place. I knew my life's duty was to serve Cio-Cio-san. And yet my eyes would brim with tears when, in the dark silence of the latest hours, a sweet girlish whisper would reach my ear.

"Suzuki-san, are you still awake? Can you dress my hair tomorrow like it was today? That very kind American is coming to hear me play my samisan again."

Just as it had been with Katsumi, I could feel her smile across the dark room, just as if it were butterfly wings brushing my cheek.

For several weeks I heard regular reports about "that very kind American". I learned that he was a Naval Officer, and that he always arrived in his crisp white uniform, with his cap tucked under his arm, and always with a small gift for Cio-Cio. He would bring her a length of silk fabric, a little bottle of perfume, an ornament for her hair. One time he arrived with a pair of beautifully painted fans, insisting with a knowing smile that one be for the young servant girl who often knelt just outside the door as Cio-Cio performed for him.

Autumn in Nagasaki again. The cold breeze up from the harbour snaked its way under the front door and stirred the long red and pink feathers in a golden vase in the entryway. The grey skies released drops of water that cascaded through the tree branches, loosening the red maple leaves as they passed. Several times a day I had to bundle up to sweep the slippery leaves from the walk. It was on one such afternoon that the visitors arrived. Cio-Cio was off at her singing lesson across town. I would usually accompany her, but this time there were too many chores around the house for me to leave.

The two men turned up the walk, stepping carefully over the leaves I had yet to sweep. I quickly bowed my head and stepped onto the uneven stones surrounding the koi pond to allow them to pass. The younger of the two was a short Japanese man, pompously dressed in a cream coloured kimono, with a beautifully embroidered haori over it, and bright blue hakama and obi. Incongruously he held a large black Western style umbrella over him to protect his clothing from the spitting rain. I peeked up as he passed and recognized him immediately. He had been at the house several times before.

The second man followed in his wake. An elegant Western gentleman in his middle years, a little on the portly side, but impeccably dressed in a conservative grey suit, with a black topcoat adorned with a wide velvet collar, a tidy bow tie, and topped with a black bowler. As he passed me, he gave me a nod and a brief smile, then followed up to the door.

I realized at that moment that I had completely lost my manners as a lady of the house, even though I was a mere servant. I rushed to join them just as the Japanese man was about to use the handle of his umbrella to jauntily rap on the door. Bowing repeatedly, I stepped past them and opened the door wide to allow them into the entryway. A swarm of red leaves caught the breeze of the open door and eddied around my hem before settling at my feet.

"Please, wait here. I will call for Junko-san," and I bowed once more as I backed out of the entrance and into Junko's office. The woman had heard us, of course, and was rising from her desk and patting her hair as I approached.

"Thank you, Suzuki. Please go to the kitchen and help the cook prepare a meal for our guests."

I waited in the office as Junko greeted the Japanese man fondly and was introduced to the Western man. I could just make out their words, but his name sounded strange to my ear. I repeated it in my head over and over to make sure I would remember. Sharpless. Sharpless.

Once they had moved into the parlour, I slipped into the kitchen and set to work. Through the partition I could hear snippets of their conversation. I tried to set my mind to cutting delicate paper-thin slices of ginger as their voices rose and fell. Most of their conversation was in English, so I only understood words here and there. I could hear the man - Sharpless - his voice rumbled deep with a pleasant American accent.

Then Junko's pitch grew louder. "But Cio-Cio-san is still just a hangyuko. Surely I could interest you gentlemen in another of the girls, a fully trained geisha, that would be far more pleasing!"

At the mention of Cio-Cio's name, my hand slipped and the knife cut deeply into my finger. Bright red blood immediately seeped out to pool around the mound of ginger slices. At my cry, cook calmly stepped to my side, picked out a slice of ginger and wrapped it around my finger. "Hold this tightly for a few minutes. The ginger will prevent infection. Then get a piece of gauze from the basket next to my needlework and dress the wound. Unfortunate that you have ruined all that lovely ginger." With a sigh, she tossed the bloody ginger into the vegetable scrap bin, gave the cutting board and my blood-stained knife a perfunctory wipe, and set about slicing bright red and white radishes instead.

The conversation in the other room had paused momentarily when they heard me cry out. I could hear Junko drop ice chips into tumblers, then pour whiskey into the glasses.

"Now, let me tell you about the lovely young women who would certainly charm your handsome associate."

"No!" I heard the Japanese man exclaim. "Lieutenant Pinkerton has grown quite fond of Cio-Cio San. It is she that he requests. Foolish woman! Why would you hesitate? He has sent us here with an excellent offer - generous compensation to you for releasing her, and a fine arrangement for Cio-Cio. Don't waste any more of our time! If the girl is not yet a full geisha, then make her a full geisha. But don't be expecting any more money for her! Our price is firm. Just sign the papers and allow our important guest to be on his way." I then heard the sound of him slamming his whiskey glass on the table. The glass shattered, and I immediately took my moment. I grabbed a basket and a rag and hurried in the room. They all turned to look at me, so I bowed deeply then swept in beside the irate Japanese to brush the broken glass and spilled whiskey into the basket. As I turned to bow at Sharpless-san again, he reached out and grabbed my wrist. I didn't notice that the cut finger from the ginger was still bleeding, and was staining the rag pink.

"You cut your hand on the glass!" he cried.

"No, sir, it's just from a little slip of a knife in the kitchen. It's nothing, sir." I blushed and pulled my hand away, then turned to Junko-san. "Shall I bring another glass for our guest, Oka-san?"

"No, thank you, Suzuki," replied Junko, as she took up a pen and ink from the sideboard. "I believe our business here is nearly complete."

I bowed again, and passed around the screen, then froze to hear the soft scratching of pen on paper. Junko rang a small bell and one of the other girls appeared from the front entry way with the gentlemen's hats and umbrella. There were murmurs of thanks and promises to discuss the details soon, then the men were out the door. I heard Junko. She sighed so deeply, I expected to find her completely deflated when I re-entered the room with a tray. She stood in the centre of the room, head bowed, brow furrowed, her hands clenched to her sides.

Three days later, we came to the full moon. Autumn was fully upon us. The endless rain rat-a-tatted on the roof, and the wind shook the last of the bright red maple leaves to swirl and gather in eddies, and sent chilly blasts through our window. I could see Cio-Cio shiver as I dressed her in her finest kimono, festooned with peacock feathers, and wrapped the brilliant green obi around her tiny waist. My cold hands fumbled several times as I fashioned her hair in multi-layered rolls, in the traditional style of hoko-shimada, and attached the new hair ornament - her latest gift from her American - in place. I lined her eyes and her eyebrows with kohl, and brushed a touch of pink onto her pale cheeks. As the final touch, I carefully coloured her generous bottom lip with red paint. When she was all ready we stopped for a moment, facing each other in our little private space, and held hands. Although she was still quaking slightly, her hands were surprisingly warm. Her face radiated calm confidence, and only the tiny shiver gave away the momentousness of this evening.

When we entered the tearoom, all the hangyoku girls were kneeling on small cushions in a circle around the room, their heads bowed. Their servant girls all knelt on the floor behind them. One empty cushion sat just inside the circle and Cio-Cio calmly walked to that and knelt. I took my place, with the other servants, behind my mistress.

After what seemed to be an eternity, I heard the swish of a silk kimono as someone entered the room. I dared to glance up through my lashes to see Junko enter the circle, followed by two of the geishas from the house. In the doorway I could see several other geishas - a few others who still lived in the house, and the rest, girls who had moved away. There was a tiny giggle from the crowd at the door, but one fierce glance from Junko silenced them.

"Cio-Cio-san, please rise." Junko's voice was gentle. There almost seemed to be an edge of regret to it. I heard Cio-Cio's skirts rustle as she rose.

Then Junko began to speak to her. She spoke so softly that, strain as I did, I could not hear the words she said. Her soft murmur would float on the air, and, each time she stopped, Cio-Cio would say "Yes" in a firm voice. This pattern continued for several minutes - murmur and Yes, murmur and Yes - and then there was silence except for the sound of kimonos moving slightly. I couldn't resist any longer. I glanced up just in time to see Junko take a fine brush from one of the geishas at her side. She dipped the brush in a pot that the other geisha held, then in one deft stroke she painted Cio-Cio's upper lip scarlet.

I looked over at the other Hangyokus kneeling in the circle. Their upper lip now looked naked and childish, like a baby's bare bottom, next to Cio-Cio and the other geishas' bright red lips. I could just make out the small scowl of jealousy on some of the faces of the girls. They were older than Cio-Cio and had been in the house longer, and clearly disapproved of what appeared to be preferential treatment.

Then I turned my eye to Cio-Cio. Her face glowed radiantly. I knew that this was not just the happiness of moving up from apprentice to master. For most young women, this would be the pinnacle of success. But in Cio-Cio-san's face I saw something else much deeper. This was the look of intense love and heart-felt anticipation of a life with her handsome American, the Lieutenant B. F. Pinkerton.

Over the next several months, Cio-Cio's training intensified. Not only was she attending her regular singing and samosan lessons but she needed to grasp the fundamentals of a tea ceremony. She learned some basic herbal remedies. She was schooled in enough knowledge of history and politics to be able to make polite conversation. And there was a secret lesson that she attended in a private room in Junka's wing of the house. Sometimes she would go in there following alone in Junka's wake. Other times, several of the older geishas would join them.

One night as we lay on our mats with the crescent moon bright outside our window I risked asking Cio-Cio about those private sessions. All I knew was that they often went on for several hours and she would sometimes come out with flushed cheeks and glistening eyes.

"What is it that you are learning in those classes, Cio-Cio-san?" I asked as nonchalantly as I could.

There was a long pause. I thought perhaps she hadn't heard me and was screwing up my courage to repeat the question when she softly replied.

"There is much about the job of being a geisha that you cannot understand, Suzuki." She stopped again and let out a deep sigh. "It is a grave responsibility to help very important men to put aside the heavy burden of their authority for a few hours. It is not all about pretty hair ornaments and musical skill."

I felt momentarily like she was rebuking me and searched my mind for a way to apologize for my forwardness.

"Forgive me, Butterfly-san," I whispered into the darkness. "I realize that your duties are wearying. I only wish to know enough to be able to best serve you. You know that I will always be your devoted and most humble servant."

"I know that, Suzuki. And I am forever grateful to you. But now I must sleep."

And with that, she turned her back to me and we never spoke openly about those sessions again.

Months passed in a blur. Every few weeks the nice British gentleman, Sharpless, came for tea. He always seemed to make a point of greeting me with kindness and I looked forward to his visits with Butterfly. Occasionally he had that terrible Goro in tow and they went into Junko's office. Butterfly's love for Pinkerton grew stronger as time passed. He came to see her whenever he could get away from his duties on his ship. He was apparently a very important man on the ship and only got away for an evening every fortnight. He always brought her a little gift, though, and would sit in one of the comfortable Western chairs in the lounge, whiskey in hand, and listen to her sing and play her samisen.

One day - it was a dark, blustery afternoon- Goro showed up at our door unexpectedly. In fact, it always seemed to be dark and blustery when he appeared. It was like he carried the weather around him like the oversized black coat he always wore. I knew from Junko's frown that she had not anticipated his arrival. He thrust his dripping coat and umbrella into my arms and marched past her into her office. She quietly told me to bring two whiskeys to them and followed him in. That Junko needed to drink during the day, and in this man's company, just reinforced my dislike of him, but I left to do as she asked. When I returned from the kitchen with two glasses and a bottle on a tray, I paused at the door to shift the tray in my hand. The door was slightly ajar. I didn't intend to eavesdrop but when I heard Junko's voice raised in anger, I stopped in my tracks, frozen into uncertainty.

"Of course the girl is a virgin. She is just a child still. And you know that Pinkerton-san had asked that she be schooled in pleasing, but that she must remain untainted for their wedding day."

Goro's high pitched voice was also too loud for the small room.

"I never made any guarantees to that American that the girl would be his. In the last few months I have received a very generous offer from Prince Yamadori for her virginity. His present wife has aged and tires him. He is willing to marry Butterfly if that is what it takes."

Junko gasped. Outside the door my hand shook so I almost dropped the glasses. I steadied them and held my breath to hear what her response would be.

"As far as I am concerned, the girl has been promised to Pinkerton-san. She truly cares for the gentleman and he treats her with the respect that a well-raised geisha deserves. There is no way I will allow Prince Yamadori…" She spit out his name with fury. "…That man to spoil one of my finest girls!"

"Frankly, madame, you really have no say in the matter. If you remember, I hold a sizeable mortgage on this house, and I will determine where the girl will go, based on the best price I can get. This is in your best interests as well, you know. You will come into a respectable portion of the girl's price. I have already spoken to Sharpless about this and he has confirmed that the amount the prince is offering is more than Pinkerton can afford, so the deal is done. You can just…"

At that moment he stopped abruptly. He must have been quite close to the door, for it quickly swung open. I stepped aside just in time to not be struck by it. He snarled at me. "Well that took long enough. What are you doing, gaping at me like that? Pour me a glass of that swill that this house passes off as whiskey."

I glanced up at Junko's reddened face and knew not to say a word. I quickly put the tray on the desk and poured him a generous amount. Ducking my head, I slipped from the room and held my breath waiting for the verbal abuse to continue. Instead I heard nothing until the glass was slammed back down onto the desk.

"I will take my leave. Trust me, I will be putting plans in place to create a marriage contract with Butterfly and Prince Yamadori. It is up to you whether you tell her or she finds out on her wedding day! Good afternoon, Madame."

I knew what I must do. Two days later I put on my only Western style clothes, a birthday gift from my mistress. I even snuck a little of Cio-Cio's rouge and eyeliner, then slipped quietly out of the house. Twenty minutes later I stood before the ornately carved oak door. The manservant looked annoyed that I had showed up unbidden and merely raised his hand to silence me once I had explained who I was. Then he closed the door in my face. I didn't know if or when he might return but one attribute of a good servant is the ability to be patient, so I bowed my head and waited.

An eternity seemed to pass before the door reopened. He still wore the same irritated expression, but this time he opened the door wider and nodded for me to enter and follow him down a dim hallway. The doors all along the way were closed, so it seemed that no natural light ever encroached on this space. Only sconces on either side of a heavy dark bureau at the end of the hall broke the darkness.

At the last door the servant quietly tapped. A muffled voice could be heard and with that I was ushered in to face Goro. He sat at a large desk, a stained cloth tucked under his chin, his cheeks stuffed and his greasy hands paused over his plate of food as he took me in. He methodically continued chewing, then took the cloth from his collar and gingerly wiped his fingers. He waved his fingers in the direction of the servant and I heard the door softly close behind me.

"Now, what gall brings the servant girl of a geisha to the home of an important man such as myself - the front door no less - to demand an audience?"

I lowered my eyes in obeisance. "Goro-san, please. I made no such demand. I merely requested a few minutes of your time to plead with you on behalf of my mistress. I may just be a servant, but I am not a stupid girl. I understand, at least a little, the ways of business affairs. I recognize that the offer from the Prince is financially preferable. But please, sir. I beg you to reconsider. Perhaps you don't realize the depth of Cio-Cio-san's affection for the American. It will break her heart to not be contracted to him."

"So, she hasn't yet been told? She did not send you to advocate on her behalf?"

"Oh no, sir. She knows nothing about your conversation with Junko-san. And if she did, she would never send me to speak to you. She may love Pinkerton-san, but, broken-hearted, she would resign herself to Prince Yamadori if her oka-san ordered it. Forgive me my boldness, but I come of my own accord." With that, I found myself blushing deeply and bowed my head even farther.

The silence sat between us. I realized that I had no choice but to play the card that I knew would be my only hope. I raised my eyes demurely with the sweet half-smile I had seen on the faces of the girls in the house as they entertained the gentlemen who visited. I resisted allowing the disgust to register on my face as I watched him daintily pick a cherry from a large bowl, inspecting it carefully for any sign of blemish. Then he turned his stare back to me as he bit into the fruit. I watched as a drip of bright red juice escaped his lips and dribbled down his chin until it finally landed on his shirt-front. The pink stain spread unnoticed as he raised his head, without breaking his gaze, and spit the seed to the floor at my feet.

"And what have you to offer me in exchange for such an enormous financial sacrifice?"

The small smile frozen on my lips, I forced my eyes from the pink stain up to meet his. In my most valiant attempt to mimic the geishas, I murmured, "Whatever would give Goro-san the greatest pleasure," and quickly ducked my head down again.

Another long silence followed. I forced myself to remain still, focused on the cherry pit at my feet.

After what felt like a lifetime, I heard him sit back in his chair.

"You have the face of a mule, so I am guessing no man has had you yet. That will give some slight satisfaction. Well, what are you waiting for? Lie down on the floor!"

I shot my eyes up to his impassive face for a moment. I realized I had passed the point of no return, and lowered myself onto the tatami. I instantly regretted the Western style blouse with its row of tiny pearl buttons down the back as my spine pressed onto them.

At that moment, the manservant thrust open the door. I saw Goro's eyes darken with disapproval for the distraction, but when he saw the leering expression on the servant's face as he looked at me prone on the floor, the master smirked and with a gloating tone said "That will be all. I am not to be disturbed."

The servant matched his lascivious expression, took one last look at my exposed ankles and shins, took up Goro's empty dinner bowl, and slipped out, quietly shutting the door behind him.

"Now," said Goro as he came out from behind his desk, "perhaps this will make the whole experience more pleasurable."

He stood over me, wiped a drop of cherry juice from his lips with his hankie, then placed the cloth over my face.

"Yes. Much better. Now, shall we get on with it?"

I had listened to the older servant girls' giggling accounts of their sexual dalliances as we gathered over the wash basins in the evenings, cleaning our mistresses' underthings. I had a basic understanding of how these things took place. I knew that this would not be the gentle love-making of a devoted suitor, but nothing could have prepared me for this. In a single move he was on his knees, hiking my skirts up to my waist and shoving my legs apart. He must have unbuttoned his pants before he stood because he instantly placed one hand firmly on my shoulder and used the other to ram himself deep inside of me. I forced myself not to cry out from the searing pain as he slammed himself in over and over again. I distantly felt the friction of the tatami mat and the sweet little pearl buttons raking against my back. At one point I heard the soft click of the door latch and realized the servant had opened the door enough to peer in. My mind registered, "he can see all the way up my bare legs," but beneath Goro's hankie, I just squeezed my eyes closed and willed myself not to faint.

After an eternity of pain, Goro gave one final thrust, let out a grunt of satisfaction, and raised himself up. He calmly removed the hankie, used it to wipe the tip of his dripping penis, then dropped it back onto my face. With the same passive expression as before, he walked back to his desk, sat down, and gingerly chose a bright red cherry from the bowl. When the juice began to drip from his lip again, he absently looked around the desk for his hankie, then at me, lying on the floor with the cloth still balled up and now resting on my chest. He sighed, shrugged and caught the drip with his finger, then licked it off, all the while admiring the half-eaten cherry in his other hand.

"You're looking a little disheveled, girl. Perhaps you should get up and rearrange yourself."

I rose unsteadily to my feet and pulled my skirts back down. Several of the pearl buttons glistened on the mat, but I dared not bend down to retrieve them. My back was on fire, I felt like I had been split in two and a sticky liquid was dripping down the insides of my legs. But I forced myself to step firmly to face him across the desk and waited until he acknowledged my scrutiny.

"So, do we have a deal? Cio-Cio-san will marry the American?"

He smiled at me for a moment, then chose another cherry from the bowl, inspecting it carefully for imperfections.

"Oh my dear, we shall see, shall we not? The Prince is making such a generous offer for the Butterfly but perhaps we can reconsider the American. I mean, really. If it is love? Who am I to deny it? I really am such a hopeless romantic."

With that he gave a dismissive little wave toward the door. On cue, the servant opened it fully and leered at my rumpled appearance as I passed him and left the house.

The walk home was a blur. I am sure I looked a shocking mess if I passed anyone. My blouse was missing enough buttons that I had to keep my arms firmly at my sides to hold it in place. My hair, which I had carefully woven into a western style arrangement, in an attempt to look more serious and mature, was now flopping loosely with each step. To have suffered through all of that and still have no assurance from the man! My cheeks burned with fury as I slipped down the alleyway behind Junko's house and quietly through the kitchen to the washing area. I know the cook saw me as I passed. I heard a tiny gasp. But I refused to pause or look her way. I took a washing pot down from its hook and filled it with hot water from the stove. After pulling the privacy curtain across, I gently peeled the ruined, blood-stained blouse from my back. I dabbed the shredded flesh as best I could with a clean cloth, and then scrubbed the sticky blood-stained rivulets that coursed down my legs.

After methodically disposing of the pink water out the window, I wrapped myself in a towel and went to our room. Fortunately, Cio-Cio was at a singing lesson that evening. I balled up my now-ruined beautiful Western outfit and stuffed them to the back of my cupboard and dressed in a soft cotton shift that I felt immediately stick to the welts on my back. It was only when I tried to remove the pins from my hair did my hands begin to shake. I gave up on my hair and curled up on my bed. But I still didn't cry.

"You idiot child! Do you realize the Sorrow you could have caused? I swear I should chop off your hair and send you to the nunnery, let the bloody Buddhists deal with your arrogance and pig-headedness! Where did you get the notion that you could just march into Goro-san's home and make demands of him? He is a despicable man but I need him, this house needs him. We need him far more than we need you, let me tell you. If I didn't owe your mother my life from when we were hangyoku..."

Junko stopped when she saw my face shoot up to meet hers. Her eyes widened when she realized what she had told me, and immediately turned to look out the window into the darkening garden. I remained frozen on my knees beside her desk. When she turned away, I dropped my face again. A pink sparkle caught my eye and I caught myself fixating on a tiny gem lying on the mat just beside her desk leg. It must have broken loose from my hair ornament when she struck me. An English style lamp with a thick glass shade of pale gold was the only light in the room as the shadows lengthened. When Junko had moved to the window, the light from the lamp cast its warm glow over me and the little pink gem. My fingers itched to reach over and pick it up. Irrationally it felt like, if I had that gem back again, everything would be all right and none of this would have happened. But I stayed still, my fingernails digging into the fabric over my knees. Finally I heard the rustle of Junko's kimono as she returned to her desk and sat in the chair before me. Still I didn't look up.

"Your mother is my niece, Suzuki. I was the youngest child in my family and she was the eldest child of my aunt's so we grew up together right here in Nagasaki. Our family was fairly well off - your grandfather was a silk merchant whose clients included the tailors of many highly respected samurai. They say he even sold silk to the Emperor's tailor occasionally.

"In those days, the samurai were the rulers and you always did whatever they told you or risked imprisonment, so one spring day the two of us - your mother and I - decided to take a walk over by the harbour to look at the cherry blossoms in full bloom. She was twelve years old and I was fourteen. It was a beautiful sunny afternoon. I remember we decided to make a real event of it for ourselves and took extra time to dress and do our hair. Mariko even slipped into her mother's room and took a little rouge to colour our cheeks. We felt like such grown-up young ladies as we paraded down the street under our parasols.

It was a lovely day. It had been raining but the sun shone for the entire afternoon, glinting off the water droplets that still clung to the blossoms, casting a magical, glittering spell over us. We were on our way home in the late afternoon, arm-in-arm, giggling with our heads close together, when I accidentally bumped into a man in the street. Honestly, we were so wrapped up in our own little world, we just didn't see him. I don't think either of us actually even looked up; we just apologized with another little giggle then started off on our way again. You can imagine my surprise when I felt a strong hand grip my arm. I stopped and looked up into the angry eyes of a samurai! He was an older man, probably in his forties, in full regalia, all in black, with his sword hanging from his belt.

Both of us felt our hearts jump into our throats. We threw aside our parasols and bowed very deeply before this imposing man. Still he held firmly to my arm. Mariko, all thoughts of her finest kimono behind her, dropped to her knees in obeisance. With his other hand he reached down and grabbed her arm and pulled her to her feet. Then without a word he turned and marched us up the street. There were a few other people on the street, workers heading home at the end of the day, shopkeepers closing up. All just bowed their heads silently as the three of us passed by. Once I tried to raise my head to meet the eyes of a butcher sitting on his front stoop, plucking a chicken. The man just shook his head and looked away, and the samurai gave me an extra hard tug to warn me to keep quiet. He led us farther and farther up the hill away from the harbor. Our home was also up the hill, but in a district very far from where we were heading now. At last he pushed us ahead of him down a narrow path in a small bamboo forest. I could hear the burbling of a fountain tucked into the garden. The path ended at a large entrance to a home entirely hidden by the foliage. He released us into a dark entranceway. It was very hard to see. No light from the setting sun found its way through the front windows of this home. He opened a screen into a back room. Here a little light came in but the hill rose sharply up behind the house, so the view in the back, instead of bamboo, was of rocks and scraggly pines climbing up out of sight. We dropped to our knees, huddled together, heads still bowed."

Junko lifted a cut crystal glass from her desk. She stared into it as she swirled the dark amber liquid. I knew she had been particularly angry with me, because Junko never drank her expensive whiskey alone. It was only brought out when the favoured gentlemen where in the house.

"What happened in that house that evening changed the course of my life, and your mother's, forever. We were led into the great room and put on display for an elderly woman. She was tiny but her power seemed to emanate from her along with the aroma of sandalwood. Her kimono was elegant, clearly made of the finest silks, and her thick white face paint and brilliant red lips masked her age. Only her skeletal, bird-like hands, revealed the truth. She sat perfectly still, her feet, tiny from years of binding, crossed demurely before her, but her coal-black eyes took in every inch of us girls as we were paraded before her.

"She told us that the Shogun has given her the divine responsibility of choosing young women to entertain the Samurai in his army, and that this was a great honour to be even considered. She explained that we would be housed and fed and trained in the arts of dancing and singing, and if we excelled that one day we might even become the wife of a great Samurai! What an exceptional honour that would be! But time was of the essence. His Excellency needed these young women to brighten the hearts of his men right away, so, no, we would not be returning home to our families. A messenger would be sent to our parents to assure them that we were safe, but our sacred duty must commence tonight!

"Mariko and I were struck dumb. We just stared at this woman. Not go home? Not see our Mama-sans? Sing and dance? It all seemed so absurd, but the little woman held our gaze. After all, we thought, we cannot refuse a direct order from the Emperor!

"So that was how we came to become hangyoku, like Butterfly is now. We trained in all the traditional ways, much like she has been doing now. But your mother has always been a free spirit and she didn't take well to the structure and the discipline.

Junko smiled for a brief moment at the memory. Her story was mesmerizing. My mother, a free spirit? Most of my life, my mother had been either pregnant or swaddling an infant. Her dress was always clean but functional. Her steps always seemed somewhat ponderous on her often swollen ankles. But with Junko's brief smile I was reminded of the way Mama-san's entire face would light up with her smile when Papa-san came through the door at the end of the day. He would often bring her home some small gift - a flower he had picked, or a fig from a low-hanging branch, or even sometimes a treasured fish cheek from a generous fisherman. She would giggle like a girl, covering her mouth with her rough-hewn hand. But if Mother had gone on to be a geisha, how did she end up in our little village, with our Father and all of us?

Junko seemed to be tracing the path of my thoughts. She took a sip of her whiskey and continued her story.

"We were set up in a house, much like this one, here in Nagasaki. At first all our time was taken up with lessons and we were never allowed to leave the house. But eventually, after a few months, we were allowed to go out in groups for fresh air. In summer the house was unbearably hot, so a gentle stroll down by the harbour was so refreshing. Of course, all the fishermen and the dock workers and the men in the shops would stop to watch us as we clattered past, with our parasols, and our wooden shoes, and our giggles. And there was one young man who always only had eyes for Mariko. He was very tall and as thin as a bamboo pole. His face was a collection of sharp angles - jaw, cheekbones, brow - but when he smiled the angles all seemed to soften to curves. Of course he never smiled at Mariko. If she turned her eye to him, he would blush, but he never looked away. But he had an easy way with the other young men on the dock. Mariko would insist that we stop to rest on a bench overlooking the boats, claiming her bound feet were hurting, or that the sun was tiring her. From there she could watch him as he loaded crates with ease, joking with the other young men, all the while sliding cautious glances up the hill to where we sat. Her favourite time to watch him though was when he was sitting quietly on a box, head bowed, brow furrowed with concentration, as he meticulously repaired a net, Even from a distance she could see his long fingers as they knotted and wove, as though he played some silent musical instrument. We teased her terribly about him! Naturally we all understood that our responsibility was to the Shogun and his Samurai so we must never, ever speak to the men in the town. But, as I said, Mariko was a free spirit. She found a way to communicate with the young man, then one morning as she and I were dressing, I sensed an odd freshness in her kimono, as if it hadn't been at rest, waiting to be worn the next day, but had been out in the night air, under the summer moon.

"That summer stretched into fall and still our lessons continued. The number of Samurai in Nagasaki seemed to multiply weekly and we were very busy every evening serving tea, sake and whiskey to the gentlemen as the geisha entertained them. Occasionally we were called upon to dance or sing for them as well. The streets seemed to swell with young men descending on the city from the surrounding villages, and often we would hear their voices late at night, brash with the exuberance of youth and alcohol, as they made their way home to their boarding houses.

"One late September night I was awoken by Mariko's firm hand on my arm. I was surprised to see her kneeling beside me, fully dressed. She put her finger to her lips to hush me, then signaled for me to follow her. The urgency in her eyes and the pallor of her cheek caused me to rise immediately. She grabbed up my blanket and wrapped it around my shoulders, then took my hand. We slipped quietly down the hall and out into the cool night. Down the road, even in the scant light of the crescent moon, I recognized the tall, slender figure of Mariko's young man from the docks. At his feet I could vaguely see what seemed to be a pile of clothes. Mariko tugged at my hand and we ran to join him. As we approached, she began to whisper, somewhat hysterically.

"'There were three of them, you see. Tetsu was just walking me home when they approached. Very drunk. Thought I was karayuka-san, a common prostitute, and offered to pay Tetsu to have their way with me. When he refused they got angry and tried to grab me. That's when Tetsu pulled his knife out, you know, the one he uses when he is repairing the nets? There was a struggle and one of the boys - that's all they were, just boys, not even men at all - grabbed me around my waist while the other two were trying to pull Tetsu away from me. He caught one of them on the nose with his elbow and blood just gushed from his nose. In the confusion that caused he managed to break free and lunged for the one holding me. I know he just meant to scare him off, to make him let go and leave us in peace. But his long arms... in the darkness... so much confusion...'

"I looked now at the young man, standing stock still, his arms hanging from his sides, and the moonlight caught a glint of the knife dangling from his fingertips, threatening to drop straight down into the bundle at Tetsu's feet. A strange and terrible mixture of scents rose up from below, acrid metal, urine and shit. I knew what I was going to find, but reached down to pull away what appeared to be a collar nonetheless. The startling white face of a boy, his eyes wide open and mouth frozen agape stared up at me. And below the face, even in the shadows, I could make out the slash across his throat and, in the black and white world of night, the inky circle of blood that surrounded him.

"Once I tore my eyes away from the bloody slash, I saw the blue and gold of his coat. The realization that this young man was from the Emperor's army woke me from my shock. I straightened up and stood between the body and Tetsu and Mariko who were clutching each other and staring at the body. I took the knife from his hand and wiped the blood off it on the blue jacket at our feet. I forced Tetsu to look at me.

"'Go home, Tetsu. Take your knife and go home. And neither of you are ever to speak to anyone about this. Do you understand?'

"He blinked slowly then took the knife in a hand that shook slightly, but didn't move.

"'Tetsu! Listen to me. Go home. Go to work tomorrow as if nothing has happened. You must do this. When the body is found, it will appear that he had an encounter with one of the Shogun's men. Go! For Mariko's sake!'

"That caught his attention. He nodded to me and took one more long look at Mariko before turning and vanishing into the shadows.

"'All right, Mariko. Let's go home too. Nothing happened tonight. Yes? You understand? It will all be all right. Let's go home.'"

Junko was still swirling the whiskey in her glass. She stopped now and took a small sip before she continued.

"I thought that would have ended the late-night trysts, but two nights later a dog's bark woke me and I looked over to see Mariko's bed disheveled and empty. With a sigh, I reached across and moved her blanket to make it look like she was burrowed under the covers. It was not uncommon for one of the geishas to come to find us during the night. If a geisha was on her moon, she could wake us to take care of her bedding. We would have to gather up the blood-stained sheet and I would wash it out right away so it didn't stain while Mariko replaced it with a clean one. With five geishas in the house and only we two hangyoku, it happened often and if one came in and found Mariko's bed empty, our Oka-san would certainly find out.

"What I didn't realize was that Oka-san kept track of our moons. She had strong superstitious beliefs about girls on their moon and food handling. She would make sure that whenever one of the geishas were bleeding, she would not perform the tea ceremony. It was a few weeks later that she called Mariko into her office. I arranged and rearranged the flowers in a vase outside the door for what seemed like hours until Mariko emerged. Even with her head bowed, I could see her tear-stained cheeks as she brushed past me. I glanced in at Oka-san and she gave a curt nod. I took that as her permission to follow my friend. I found her curled on her bed, tears still silently falling on her pillow. After a few minutes, her cracked barely audible voice rose up to me.

"'Junko, I have made such a terrible mistake. I had such dreams of my life as a geisha. But Tetsu... I love him so much... Now I have lost them both. Where am I going to go? Oka-san was very fair, but I will have to leave. And Tetsu won't want me. Not now. What can I do? My life is over!'

"'Why would you have to leave? Can you not just tell Oka-san you won't see Tetsu any more? I know that would be hard, but you can still continue your training. You can still be a geisha. Why couldn't you? This seems so unfair! I will go talk to her!'

"Mariko took my hand before I could stand. 'No, Junko, you don't understand. I am pregnant. My moon hasn't come in three months. I didn't realize it, but Oka-san noticed. She told me to stay in our room until she decides what she is going to do. She told me the herbalist has medicine that can make the baby die. But I am still not going to be a geisha. I am of no value to her if I am not a virgin. I don't want the baby to die but how can I manage on my own with a baby? What can I do?'

"She fell silent again. My mind raced. Mariko, your mother, was my dearest friend. Perhaps my only friend.

"' It will be all right, Mariko. Just do as Oka-san says. Stay here. I will come back soon.'

With that I left the room. I took an umbrella from the stand in the entryway and slipped out into the rainy afternoon, heading for the harbour.

It took a while to find Tetsu. With the heavy rain, most of the dock workers had taken refuge in the fish shops and the canneries. My feet were drenched when I finally located him in a tiny tea house. The steamy smell of strong tea, ginger, fish and men assaulted me as I brushed past the curtain and entered the tiny shop. There were far too many men, large and small, young and old, most wearing heavy aprons smeared with fish blood, all seeming to talk at once. I caught snippets of conversation about the weather, the latest American ship to dock, and the politics of Emperor versus Shogunate. There was a brief pause in the babble as I shook out my umbrella and brazenly entered this male domain. I searched the faces until I found Tetsu tucked in a corner with three other young men. He cradled his cup of tea and looked up when the room momentarily fell silent.

"Early the next morning, before the rooster had even signalled the coming dawn, Mariko, Tetsu and I met on the road, not far from where the body of the young man had lain. Mariko wore her simplest kimono, so as not to draw attention. In her arms she clutched a fabric bundle tied together with twine. In it was a few personal items, a paper packet of rice and seaweed, what little money she and I had been saving with our dream of one day becoming okas ourselves, with houses of our own, and a note. I had written to my cousin, who lived in a village down the coast - your village - asking him to do what he could to help Tetsu to find work and a home for himself, the young girl who would become his bride, and their unborn child. The rain had slowed to a drizzle and the air was brisk with the promise of winter and before any of us could change our minds I hugged my dearest friend, turned away and walked briskly back to our house. That was the last I saw of her. My cousin wrote to me, many months later, to say that they had settled in the village, that Tetsu hoped to open a small tailor shop, using the skills he had acquired sewing fishing nets, and that Mariko had given birth to a healthy baby girl. That would have been, I am guessing, your older sister? The next time I laid eyes on Mariko was when she arrived at my doorstep two years ago with you and your other sister in tow."

With that Junko downed the last of her whiskey. Her eyes, still filled with the past, met mine. For a brief moment that past flowed between us like our breath passed air back and forth, then it was gone and she was once again the stern mistress.

"You are lucky that Goto-san did not demand your removal from our household. He seemed more amused than annoyed by your visit. He told me that you marched in, demanding he toss aside a perfectly good business deal for the sake of 'love'. Really, child, what were you thinking?"

Bowing my head again, my voice barely a whisper, I asked, "And what did he say occurred after that?"

"Only that he allowed you to say your piece, then offered to have his man-servant escort you home. He said you rather rudely refused his offer, but seemed to understand that he had no intention of changing his mind."

I looked up in surprise. My face flushed bright pink and I burst out, "What? He is still making the marriage agreement with the Prince? I thought sure he had promised..." My voice faltered at my own foolishness.

"No, Suzuki, he made no such promise to you. Why would he? His world is one of business dealings, American dollars, important men. There is no room there for the childish wishes of a mere servant girl. Now I hope you have learned your lesson. For the rest of this week you will rise early in the mornings to do Cook's bidding. Oh, and Suzuki, under no circumstances will you mention any of this to Butterfly. She will find out soon enough the direction of her life."

I bowed deeply and backed out of the room. With the door closed behind me, I took a deep breath as emotions swirled around me. Gratitude that at least Goro had not revealed the lengths I went to in order to seal a deal. Fury that he clearly never intended to keep his word. Mortification at my own naiveté. And now, through all of that, the terrible fear that, like my mother, I could find myself with child and tossed aside, but, unlike my mother, with no loving husband to begin life anew.

The following weeks crawled along as if I were tethered to a sack of rocks that I dragged behind me with each step. Every time I was sent out on errands, I would take a route that passed as many shrines as possible, stopping at each one to make an offering and say a prayer. Each morning I would kneel at my own makeshift shrine to chant and sit in silent prayer that, like Cio-Cio, my fate had not been sealed by the machinations of Goro. When fear would stir like butterflies in my belly, I caught my breath, imagining that it was in fact the stirrings of a new life within me. Cio-Cio was naturally surprised at my apparent new-found attachment to the gods.

"What on earth has come over you, Suzuki? What could possibly be troubling you so to make you as reverential as the nuns in the temple? Our life is wonderful! One day soon a date will be set for me to marry my Pinkerton-san. He grows more and more attentive and generous with each visit. Then he will set us up in our own home and... Wait! Is that your concern? That I will not bring you with me when I go to live with my husband? Of course, you silly thing! I would never leave you behind! You are not just my servant, you are my dearest friend and will be until the day I die."

She hugged me close and in my mind I feared that she would feel the fullness of my belly.

When Cio-Cio came into her moon that month, it set off a new panic in me. We were so close, so in tune with each other, that our moons, like simultaneous waves lapping onto the beach, governed by the same tide, usually arrived together. For two days, she took to her bed, not permitted to take part in any of the entertaining activities of the house, a door firmly shut between her moon and the gentlemen. I was kept busy out in the yard, washing a constant succession of bloody rags. Lines strung up over the gardens were festooned with the flapping pink flags, like testaments to Cio-Cio-san's unblemished allure.

The wounds on my back slowly healed. I was grateful to not have the daily reminder of that horrible encounter every time my kimono shifted slightly on my body. Cio-Cio's moon passed and she returned to her routines of lessons in the day and entertaining in the evenings. She left early one morning to walk to her music lesson, so I turned to my shrine. I was kneeling, praying to the gods to forgive me, when I felt a familiar tug deep in my belly. I barely had time to get to my feet and retrieve a pad before the blood poured from my body in thick red-black clots. The cramping that followed was debilitating, crippling. Wave over wave flowed through me and the blood gushed out of my body at such a rate that I had to lie down on the floor with light-headedness. I gathered my skirts up and placed clean pads under me, but still the red stream pooled on the floor and tinted my hems pink. I wept exhausted tears as the waves of pain pounded the shore of my body for what seemed like hours until I finally retreated into sleep. When I awoke, the light in the room had shifted toward dusk and I realized that Cio-Cio would be returning soon. The storm of pain had receded, leaving me with a deep ache and a sticky black mess all around me that smelled like death. I eased myself up off the floor and peeled away the cloths that clung to my buttocks and between my legs. Quickly disrobing, I dipped a clean rag in the wash basin and wiped myself off, leaving a pale pink stain in rivulets down my legs. I donned a fresh kimono, wrapping the obi as loosely as I could around my aching belly. I gathered up all the bloody rags and took them outside, being careful to not be seen by the Cook as I passed the kitchen. As hard as I scrubbed the floor, the stain, like a pink shadow thrown by my lower body remained as if to haunt me. Had this been the child conceived in hatred with Goro? Or was this merely the gods punishing me for my impudence in thinking that I, a person with no value in this world, could carry any influence in the matters of love. I quickly returned to my altar and vowed to never know such arrogance again, but would strive to be only the humble servant that I was.

My resolve didn't last long. Barely a week later, Cio-Cio burst into our room as I was chanting. She fussed around behind me, clearly impatient for me to finish my prayers. When I rang the bell three times and blew out the candle, she exclaimed, "Finally! Honestly, Suzuki, I think you spend more time with those gods of yours than you do with me! Now come on! Get your wrap. We have an errand to run."

I listened to the rain beating down on the roof. "Now? That is a cold rain coming down out there. Can it wait for an hour or so? Maybe the weather will change and we won't get soaked."

"No! We have to go right now! Just bundle up and bring your umbrella. You'll be fine. What is it the Americans say? 'You're not made of sugar. You won't melt.'" She giggled excitedly and, taking my hand, pulled me out the door.

We climbed for what seemed like miles. We had to cling to each other, partly to avoid slipping on the muddy path, and partly because we were constantly being forced off the path by large groups of shogunate soldiers. They seemed to be filling the city, pouring down the hill from their encampment high above Nagasaki. Still Cio-Cio said not a word. Finally she stopped at a small park next to a settlement of large new homes overlooking the harbour.

Cio-Cio suddenly became intensely animated. She was like a puppy who smelled the arrival of its master. A moment later two men, their collars pulled up and hats tugged low against the rain, came up behind us.

"Butterfly!" one called out.

"Pinkerton-sama! You're here!"

The American's white naval cap seemed to glow in the gloomy day as if a beam of sunlight shone just for him. The second man stepped closer and I felt a smile touch my lips as I realized that it was Sharpless.

The two men came to meet us. Pinkerton took Cio-Cio's tiny hands in his and pressed his lips to them, first one, then the other. It was such an intimate gesture than I felt I needed to look away. Sharpless caught my eye and broke the silence by saying, "Miss Suzuki, we passed a tree just back there that I don't think I have ever seen before. The bark seems to be flaking off in sheets. Perhaps you might recognize it and tell me what it is?" And with that, he took my arm and gently led me along the path out of earshot of the couple.

We stopped next to a tree, whose leaves lay thickly on the ground in varying shades of red and brown. The bark was flaking away from the trunk.

"Ah," I said, "that is called a Paper Bark Maple. Do you not have this tree in America?"

"No. I mean we have maples, of course, but not like this one. Nor do we have those beautiful ones with the bright red trunks. Our maples grow much taller than yours here, and in the autumn the leaves not only turn red, but quite vibrant yellow and orange as well. Whole forests of these glow as if they are lit from within."

"I would very much like to see that one day. Perhaps I could come to America and you could show me." I felt my face turn as crimson as the maple leaves at my feet at blurting out such a presumptuous idea.

"I would be honoured to show you," Sharpless replied, and I was pleased to see his cheeks had turned rosy as well. "Now we should join the others. I don't believe it would be considered appropriate for them to be out here without chaperones before they are wed."

He took my arm again but I stopped him before he could lead me back. I had been trying to find a way to ask him if he knew about the arrangement that Junko was making with the Prince behind Pinkerton's back, but that thought only brought back terrible memories of my meeting with Goro. I didn't want to spoil the day, or chance him removing his grasp of my arm, but I knew I couldn't keep it to myself any longer.

"Sharpless-san," I started.

"Please, Suzuki, could you call me Bart? That is my first name. Sharpless reminds me of my unpleasant teachers at school."

"All right. Bart-san, I have terrible news that I must share with you."

He turned to me, his face full of concern.

"The other day, Goro-san came to the house to see Junko-san." I hesitated. My heart was breaking for my dear friend and the man she loved.

"What did that wretched man want this time?"

"He came to tell her that Prince Yamadori had made a higher offer for Cio-Cio's hand and that he was breaking his bond with Pinkerton-san and was demanding that he marry the Prince. I didn't mean to eavesdrop on the conversation! I was outside the office door and his voice was very loud. I didn't know what to do. The Prince is not a nice man like Pinkerton-san. He won't treat her well, and he divorced his last wife only because she grew too old for his liking, and Cio-Cio will be so unhappy, and..." My words finally ran out with my breath and I just stood looking sadly into his eyes.

"Butterfly - Cio-Cio-san - she doesn't know?"

"Oh no, Bart-san! I couldn't tell her. I know Junko-san will tell her soon. Oh! She is going to be so very unhappy! I just don't know what to do!"

Sharpless gently placed one hand on my cheek, just for a moment.

"You don't need to do anything, Suzuki. Please don't let yourself be too upset by this. I will talk to Pinkerton right away and we will make sure that Goro doesn't get away with this. That bast... that terrible man will not renege on the promise that he made."

He waited with me for another minute, giving me time to take control of my emotions again, then steered me back down the path with a determined step.

Cio-Cio and Pinkerton stood very close together. Pinkerton's head was bent low next to the lovely geisha's ear and they were quite lost in conversation as we approached. At the sound of the leaves under our feet, he looked up and his face broke into an enormous grin. He spoke rapidly in English, most of which I couldn't understand, but, seeing the confusion on my face, Sharpless deftly translated.

"He said that he was just explaining to Butterfly that this is where he wishes to build their beautiful home. The sky is so foggy it doesn't do justice to the view down to the harbour. Many of the homes that have been built up here already are owned by Americans as well, so they will be right at home here."

Cio-Cio smiled and nodded, and added, "Of course you will live here as well, Suzuki! I will need your help to manage such a large, wonderful home."

"It will be a lovely place," I managed in my broken English to Pinkerton, who also smiled and nodded. With that, we all seemed to have run out of things to say. Sharpless took out his pocket watch and suggested that perhaps we should get back to Junko's before it grew dark.

"Would you like us to escort you back down the hill?" he asked politely.

Before Cio-Cio could jump at the opportunity to spend more time with her American, I said firmly, "Thank you but no. We can manage the path just fine. It was very nice to see you again." And I took a step toward Cio-Cio. As much as I too was enjoying the presence of the gentle, kind Sharpless, I couldn't risk us being seen together on the road below. I thought it would be just our luck to run into Goro or his hateful servant and have him see that Junko had not yet broken the dreadful news of their contract to Cio-Cio.

I felt like I had to hold firmly to Cio-Cio's arm as we walked for fear that she would lift off the ground and take flight. She was bubbling over with so many words, far more, I am sure, than she and Pinkerton actually exchanged.

"The house, Suzuki! The house! It is going to be magnificent! Big and solid like a real American home! Two storeys! Indoor plumbing! Electric lighting! He even told me about the bed he will get for us. It will be huge and so high off the ground I will need a step to get up onto it. And as soft as a cloud! With silk sheets and a dozen pillows! And all the rooms will have enormous windows looking down on the harbour so we can look down upon his powerful ship and all the sailors under his command! Oh, Suzuki! We will be so happy here!"

Over and over I told myself that I needed to tell her the truth, but Bart-san had been clear that he would take care of it, and I trusted him. I would hold my tongue and pray that he would find a way to protect her heart from pain.

Once again, weeks slipped past. Cio-Cio's days were filled with music lessons, English lessons, tea service lessons, and those other lessons that occurred behind closed doors. I now had a better idea of what the girls were being schooled in during those sessions, and I spent many hours praying to the gods that she never experience the same physical and emotional pain that I had faced since that one occurrence on Goro's floor. The wounds on my back and deep inside of me may have healed, but the shame, the blind rage, that rose up in me, unbidden and unwelcome, and utterly unexpected, most days, drove me back more and more to my little altar to pray for peace, and for an unlikely but longed-for outcome.

There was no sign of Pinkerton. I feared that Bart had told him the news and his response had been to walk away and not attempt to fight for his Butterfly's hand. Perhaps he was already making arrangements with Goro to meet another young geisha who could become his wife instead. Perhaps he had decided to give up completely on the idea of a Japanese wife, and was instead preparing to return to America. My mind swam with every possible horrible outcome.

We were into the depth of winter. Rain pelted the roof day and night. The little stove in the tea room and the one in the kitchen did little to fend off the cold and the dampness that seemed to pervade the house. It was hard to tell day from night as the heavy clouds completely masked the sun. Only Cio-Cio's schedule of lessons verified the days. Even the gentlemen seemed to have vanished like the sun. Most evenings, the geishas would be dressed in their finest kimonos, their faces painted like dolls, and they would end up all sitting together near the stove, whiling the time away with games of Go or folding paper into paper cranes for good luck. At least then laughter filled the house. Even Junko seemed more at ease on those evenings. Although she never joined in on the games, and would frown disapprovingly if one of the girls did an impersonation of one of their regular guests, she would pause in the doorway, teacup in hand, and survey her girls with the tiniest smile on her lips.

It was on one such evening that there was a sharp knock on the door. The laughter stopped immediately as everyone leapt to their feet. All of us servants rushed to put away the games that were strewn around the room and the geishas quickly checked each other's hair and make-up. Junko happened to be in the doorway leading to her office at that moment so she waved me away as I hurried to get the door. She handed me her teacup, patted her own perfectly placed hair and opened the door.

A blast of cold damp air seemed to knock her back a step and wet, bright red maple leaves swirled around her before sticking to the stone flooring of the entryway. I couldn't see who was out there but Junko was clearly surprised. The light was dim away from the lamps brightly filling the tea room and a large figure stepped over the threshold. It was then I saw the white naval cap.

"Oh, Pinkerton-san! It's you!" I exclaimed, before catching a fierce look of reprisal from Junko. I bowed low and stayed like that until I could see by his movements that he had taken off his coat. Even then I only looked up long enough to take his dripping coat and cap from him. But still, I saw the tiniest of winks. I backed away quickly, then ran to hang his coat by the kitchen stove to dry and to find Cio-Cio.

I found her in the kitchen, checking her make-up in the small mirror. Like many of the girls, I could see she was disappointed that a guest had shown up. We so rarely got a chance to be all together - to laugh, and play games, and just be the children we all still were.

"Cio-Cio! It's Pinkerton-san! He's here! He has come to talk to Junko! Maybe everything is going to be all right after all!"

"Of course everything is going to be all right, Suzuki. Why wouldn't it be? You saw the place where he is building a house for me. What would make you say something like that?"

I quickly bowed to her, to hide the bright flush of my cheeks. I had held the news about the Prince inside for so long. Now with that silly slip of the tongue, would I have to confess it to her?

"Well, it's just that... You know... Pinkerton-san has been away for such a long time... And I just worried..."

Cio-Cio's face lit up like a golden sunrise. She grabbed me in a tight hug, then let out a little "Oh" and ran back to the mirror to make sure she hadn't smeared her make-up or mussed her hair. Then she looked back at me, put her hand to her mouth and let out that carefree giggle I had heard every day since the day we met.

"Don't be so silly. He's been away because he is very important with a great many responsibilities. He's here now, right? I think he took the first moment he could get away from that ship of his to come straight here and talk to Junko about a wedding date!"

She ran out into the entryway, but found the door to Junko's office firmly shut. She put her hand on the doorknob, and for a moment I thought she would brashly march in there, unbidden. No one ever did that. Ever.

Fortunately, she paused there and looked around, as if she had found herself in an unfamiliar room. Then, with a small smile, she walked over to the front door of the house, gracefully knelt down beside it, facing Junko's door. She placed her hands delicately in her lap. She would wait.

And, of course, if my mistress was to wait, then so must I. I moved over to the doorway to the tea room and knelt, placing myself so that I could also see the closed door, but could also watch Cio-Cio. The low, indecipherable rumble of voices could be heard.

Over the voices, I listened to the ticking of the clock on the small table next to the office door. Behind me, I heard the occasional rustle of silk. All the geishas were on cushions in the tea room. They had no idea what was going on, but they knew that one of their own was feeling distress, so they were silently kneeling, holding vigil with Butterfly.

An hour later, most of the girls had quietly slipped away to bed. When I glanced over my shoulder, I could see that someone had dimmed the lamps in there and a few of the girls had curled up on their cushions like royal kittens. I feared for Cio-Cio's health. Even from across the room, I could feel the cold draught that whistled under the front door. Although she was clutching her hands tightly together, I could see them ever-so-slightly shaking.

Twenty minutes after that, just as I was about to get to my feet to at least find a wrap to cover Cio-Cio, the office door swung wide. Junko was holding it open. She spotted me first, and frowned. Then she turned her eyes to Cio-Cio, kneeling with her pale face bowed. Junko caught my eye and a small smile twinkled in her eye.

"Butterfly? Child, would you join Pinkerton-Sama and me?"

I rose stiffly and hurried to help Cio-Cio to her feet, but she rose up gracefully as if she had only just knelt down, nodded to Junko and passed by into the room. Junko glanced once more at me, then began to close the door, but left it just slightly ajar. I realized the gift she was giving me, rushed to a spot next to the door but out of sight, and knelt once again.

There was the rustling of fabric as they seated themselves in the three chairs in Junko's office. After a pause, I heard Junko's voice.

"Butterfly, Goro has received a very, very generous offer for your hand. From Prince Yamadori."

I heard Cio-Cio exclaim, then the words poured out of her.

"Oh Junko-Sama, please. You know I have never been disobedient to you. I have always been dutiful to you. But..."

Pinkerton's calm voice cut in.

"Butterfly, wait. Listen to what Junko has to say."

"As I said, the Prince has been exceptionally generous in his offer. Goro and I both agree that it would be foolish to not accept. Not to mention the Prince's standing in Nagasaki. He has assured Goro that there would be additional benefits for the house and the other girls if we accept his proposal."

I felt tears well up in my eyes. Poor Cio-Cio. What cruelty to have to receive this news with the man she truly loves and wishes to marry sitting right at her side! Once again, Pinkerton cut in.

"Butterfly, you need to understand that I am not a wealthy man. I am a mere officer in the American Navy. Although I expect my rank to improve, and with it my salary, I do not have a prince's inheritance to draw from. When I found out that the Prince was still vying for your hand, I went to Goro to ask the amount he was offering. It was a staggering sum! And, well, you can imagine that Goro was anxious to agree, but I begged him to wait, to hold off on accepting for just a short while. I must admit that I had real doubts that I could ever find a way to match his offer."

Cio-Cio let out a tiny sob, then, with a breaking voice, said, "Pinkerton-Sama, I understand. You must not throw all your hard-earned money on a lowly geisha. Do not blame yourself. I will go with Prince Yamadori, but I will never forget you."

Junko's voice was stern. "Child, let the gentleman finish speaking!"

"As I said, I asked Goro for time and he at first refused, until I reminded him of the number of American sailors who pay visits to his various geisha houses. Then he had a change of heart. I immediately sent a message home to my bank in America, asking for a loan. Since then I have been waiting for a response. Every day I watched for a telegraph with news one way or the other. I didn't want to come see you until I knew if I could come up with the money. Finally today, I got word. I went to Goro immediately with my counter-offer. It was only slightly more than the Prince's offer, but it was enough."

By this time, my tears had turned to tears of joy. I heard Cio-Cio's exclamation as she realized what Pinkerton was telling her.

"But, my dear Butterfly," he continued, a sober tone in his voice. "I am not sure this is the best choice for you. The Prince can offer you the palatial home you deserve. A house full of servants. Beautiful clothing and elegant parties." There was a pause and when he spoke again I could hear the shame in his voice. "I am a mere officer in the American Navy. I was not born into great wealth like the Prince. This money to Goro has stretched me financially to my very limit. I'm afraid it would mean that I could not build you that grand home high over the city. I would be forcing you to live a much simpler life than I could hope for you."

"Where would we live though, Pinkerton-san?" Cio-Cio's voice sounded so worried, it took all my restraint to not run in there to her side.

"I promise I will find us a small home. With luck, it will still have a view of the harbour, but it will not be in that neighbourhood of the other Americans."

"And Suzuki?"

"Of course, Suzuki will come with you. And I will hire a man-servant to help around the house, and to keep you safe whenever I am deployed back to sea. I have looked at a couple of choices, and, now that Goro has seen the colour of my money, he is helping me to search. But Butterfly, please think carefully about this. Think with your mind, not your heart. The Prince might not be your heart's first choice, but he will offer you a life of luxury."

The silence that followed seemed interminable. I finally couldn't bear it any longer and twisted my body around to peek through the crack in the door. Just as I did, I heard the rustle of silk and saw Cio-Cio throw herself to her knees beside Pinkerton. I could see the tears on her cheeks as she grabbed for his hand.

"Pinkerton-san! Please don't force me to marry the Prince! Please tell me that you want me to be with you! How can you tell me to not listen to my heart? My heart has been yours since the day we met! I would live in a tinker's shack, as long as it was with you."

Beyond Cio-Cio I saw the briefest shadow cross Junko's face but she quickly masked it as Pinkerton turned to her.

"Junko-san, if you are also in agreement, then I will make the final contract with Goro. Butterfly, I will send word to you as soon as I have found a home for you to move to. Then, once you have settled in there, we will marry. I must admit that I find the constant rains of Nagasaki's winters terribly dreary. A spring wedding will be just the thing, don't you think?"

Once again, the weeks slipped by. Cio-Cio intensified her English lessons and demanded that I join her. "The servant of an American wife surely must be able to speak English," she said. "How will you manage when Pinkerton-san takes us home to the United States of America with him?" So together we studied. A house boy, young Fujio, had to escort us to and from our lessons. The streets had become terribly dangerous. The Emperor was sending more and more soldiers into the city and skirmishes between them and the Shogunate seemed to be occurring on every street corner. Passing the doorways of drinking establishments, raised voices filled with anger and foul words assaulted our ears. One late afternoon, returning home from a class, two groups of men were arguing on the path directly in front of us. The path was narrow and there was no route around them, so we stopped and Fujio placed himself in front of us. On one side, men were calling the Emperor every possible vile name. On the other, the Shogunate was derided for being power-hungry tyrants who roamed the streets raping and pillaging. Then a punch was thrown and the mass of men collided in on each other. Fists flew. We watched in horror when a glint of metal flashed in the final low rays of the sun. A man fell. A dark pool of blood began to form around him like a shadow on the ground. The assailant and his friends pulled back, then one took his arm and dragged him away up the path. Someone knelt beside the fallen man and tried to stop the bleeding, but there was so much blood. It just seemed to pump out of him as from a well. Even from a distance, I could see the moment when the life force left his body. His companions stood above him in shock and grief, then together they gathered up his body and began to walk toward us. We pressed up to the wall next to the path to let them pass. The sharp stones dug into my back as Fujio once again placed himself between us and the entourage. Even so, I couldn't help but see the rage in the men's faces and the slow drip of blood that followed in their wake.

Only once the path was completely clear again did we venture home. We had to hug the wall and tiptoe single-file past the ugly pool of blood. Cio-Cio and I clung to each other's arms and poor young Fujio looked very pale as he courageously led us along.

With Cio-Cio's upcoming nuptials, she was required less and less to entertain and perform for the gentlemen guests in the evenings. Most nights she and I huddled close around a lamp in our room and strained our eyes over delicate embroidery on a new white kimono Junko had purchased for her wedding. Cio-Cio had begged to be allowed to wear a Western style wedding dress like she had seen in pictures on the wall of one of the shops in town. Junko gently informed her that such a dress was far beyond her ability financially, even for her beloved Butterfly. The white kimono was lovely, but Cio-Cio insisted on adding an intricate design of cranes and orchids and birds that she imagined were what American eagles looked like. To me they looked more like swans, but Cio-Cio was happy, and that was all that mattered.

Winter finally began to give away to the coming of spring. The tiniest blush of green appeared on the cherry trees. The breeze coming up from the harbour was gently warmed by the sun. Although the streets and paths still seemed to teem with the stern faces of men in uniforms of all kinds - the Emperor's, the Shogunate, and the resolute young American sailors - more and more of the people of Nagasaki ventured out to reclaim their city. Families strolled the walkways around the harbour. Women bustled in and out of the shops with baskets full of bags of rice, paper-wrapped fish and delicate bamboo shoots. The warmer days seemed to bring a renewed sense of hope and peace.

It was on one such morning that a cart arrived at the house. Two workmen came to the back door and informed cook that they were here to deliver

Butterfly and her belongings to her new home. There was a sudden flurry of chaos and all the servant girls were called to action to help me pack up all our personal items for the men to carry out to the cart. I felt the sting of tears as I looked around the bare room that she and I had shared since we were mere children. I watched as Cio-Cio, now a mature young woman of sixteen, hugged each of the other geishas then stepped up to face Junko. Junko gently placed her hands on Cio-Cio's cheeks.

"You are now the lady of your own house, Butterfly. I am proud of the woman you have become and I will be honoured to stand in your presence on the day of your wedding. Never forget to respect and obey your husband-to-be. He is your master now and you must answer only to him and no other."

Cio-Cio's smile lit up her face. She took hold of Junko's hands and pressed them to her lips. Then she turned and walked out the front door of the house that had been our home and graciously waited for a workman to offer his hand to help her to the seat of the cart.

Calling out "Goodbye" and "I will miss you", I rushed to follow her and was helped up to sit on the back of the cart and we started the bumpy journey to our new home.

The trip was surprisingly long. I leaned my back against the hampers that held Cio-Cio's wardrobe and tried my best to keep my dangling legs from being splashed by the mud that sprayed off the wheels as the cart rolled through one deep puddle after another along the track. I tried to ignore the red-brown splatters that dotted the hem of my kimono. I watched the scenery pass away before me as we rode high over the city then circled back to drop down on the far northern side of the harbour. The air felt cooler here, where the sun less frequently graced the land. We seemed to have left the city behind. There were no signs of homes or gardens here and I began to worry that perhaps the workmen were lost when I heard the driver call out to his mule and the animal pulled to a stop.

The man in the back with me jumped down and offered a hand for me to step off to the muddy path. It wasn't until I came around the cart to Cio-Cio's side that I spotted the small house standing alone ahead of us. Bamboo grew close around it, as it attempting to reclaim the land. Beyond the side of the house the ground seemed to drop off as if we were at the end of the world. The thatching on the roof was a bit thin in places but looked water-tight.

The wide double doors at the front of the house swung open. Sunlight seemed to flow out from the room behind as framed in the doorway stood dear Sharpless. He had removed his jacket and rolled up his shirt sleeves. Both Cio-Cio and I let out a breath of relief at the sight of him. He took long strides down the leaf-strewn path to greet us, all the while hurriedly pushing down his sleeves. In his wake followed the sweet, brave house-boy Fujio, scurrying to keep up while attempting to help Sharpless into his coat.

Sharpless reached us just as he was fastening the last button. He bowed respectfully to Cio-Cio. "Butterfly-Sama, welcome to your new home. We were hoping to get a few more things tidied up before you arrived, but Pinkerton was so anxious to get you set up here. Young Fujio here has been working day and night cleaning and doing repairs."

Fujio flushed bright pink and bowed deeply. Then in a rush of words he said, "Cio-Ci... um, Butterfly-san, let me take care of moving all your belongings in. Please go in and look around. Please tell me if there is anything that displeases you. Junko-san has told me that I am to stay here with you and be your house-boy here and I promise I will take care of everything and will make sure you are safe and happy here. Until Pinkerton-san is here with you, of course. Then it will be his job to keep you safe and happy. But I will still be here after that too. I will be here for as long as you want me here. I am your loyal servant, Butterfly-san." He finally ran out of breath, flushed and bowed again.

Cio-Cio smiled and bowed back with a look of kindness and appreciation, which only made him blush redder. Then he scurried around to the back of the cart and started barking orders at the two workmen. Sharpless led the way back up the path, bending occasionally to pick up a branch that had fallen and blocked our way and tossing it aside.

Inside the front room I realized why Sharpless had been so brightly lit in the doorway. The room was small and mostly bare but, across from the front door, another set of large doors stood open out to a tiny garden with a sharp drop-off at the end. From the doorstep you could look down beyond the cliff to the harbour. It looked strange and foreign from this angle. I had never seen it from the north. The cliff obscured much of the docks and all of the town, but in clear view was the American ship. Pinkerton's ship.

The garden was entirely wild but in one corner a small cherry tree struggled to push up past the overgrown weeds. It is south-facing, I thought. This will be my garden. I can make this beautiful for Cio-Cio.

I realized that Cio-Cio had stopped in the middle of the room. Both Sharpless and I turned at the same moment to look at her. Tears were flowing down her cheeks. The salty streams left tiny rivulets in her white face paint and the sight broke my heart.

"Cio-Cio, you'll see. We will make this place beautiful for you. I will grow lovely flowers to place in vases in every room and burn that sweet incense that you so like. And listen. Even on this cold grey day, you can hear the birds of spring singing out in anticipation of beautiful days ahead."

"Oh Suzuki! Don't be silly! These are tears of joy. Don't you understand? I have everything I have ever wanted. I love this house because it is proof that my Pinkerton really does love me! And soon we will be married and we will live a long life as husband and wife. And I will bear him beautiful children who will grow up to be as smart and handsome as he, or as content and lucky as I am."

She gave me a quick hug, then gave me her hankie so I could repair the damage to her make-up. In a flash, her mood had changed again, and she struck out to inspect the rest of her new home, in all regards now the lady of the house. She admired her bedroom, with more large windows that let in light but were masked by a privacy screen of bamboo growing outside. She reached down and tested the softness of the sleeping pad, then let out a little giggle of modesty. She admired the fact that, even in such a small house, there was a separate chamber pot closet, with a small high window that even opened. She inspected the cooking room and the small chambers for me and Fujio, constantly checking with me to make sure that it was all to my liking.

Looking at my own little bedroom, I felt a whirlwind of emotions. I had never in my life had a room that was just mine. My parents' home had been so filled with children that I couldn't remember a time when there weren't at least four of us in a room, and a bed that I had always shared with my sister Katsumi. And since arriving at Junko's house five years ago I had grown from child to woman sleeping by the side of my mistress.

I also noticed that, even though the room was small, it was graced by Sharpless' kind gestures. The sleep pad was as generously soft as Cio-Cio's own. The walls smelled pleasantly of fresh paint. And in one corner of the room, in a spot that would catch the morning light, he had set a lovely cushion before a low shelf, clearly a place for my altar. His thoughtfulness seemed endless. I realized he was standing behind me in the doorway and when I turned to him, his dear face was filled with such a childlike desire to please, I almost laughed with joy. I composed myself and bowed deeply to him, saying softly, "Thank you,

Sharpless-Sama. Everything is perfect. I know Butterfly and her Pinkerton will be very happy here. As am I."

Back in the front room, Sharpless smiled at Cio-Cio. "Butterfly-san, I will leave you and Suzuki-san now to let you get settled in. Is there anything I have not thought of that you need in your new home?"

She looked around the room. " A proper gentleman's armchair. With a footstool and a small table," she said. "My husband needs a place to rest and drink his scotch at the end of his work day."

He nodded. "Of course. I will arrange for those to be brought up here within the week. And I will return soon to make sure there is nothing else you need."

He bowed to us both. Fujio appeared with his hat and umbrella. Sharpless patted the boy's shoulder fondly. "Take care of the ladies, Fujio. You are the man of the house when Pinkerton-san is away."

Fujio pulled himself up a little taller and nodded solemnly. Then Sharpless headed out the door and made his way down the path. I watched him as he walked off down the road, heading back into town, his umbrella tucked under his arm and his hands clasped behind his back, and felt a little tug on my heart.

The days and weeks slipped by in a flurry of activity. I unpacked all our belongings, carefully hanging up Cio-Cio's kimonos and laying out her hair ornaments and make-up on a dressing table in her room. Sharpless had quite generously stocked the kitchen and I was grateful for the many hours I had worked at Cook's side so I was able to provide simple but tasty meals for us all. Fujio proved to be a clever assistant in the kitchen, chopping and stirring, then cheerfully humming to himself over the wash basin cleaning up after our meals. He had discovered a footpath leading down the hill from the corner of the garden. It was a shorter, but steeper, route down into town. Once a week the boy and I would pick our way down to fill our baskets with supplies. Before one such trip, Cio-Cio had pressed a few coins into my hand with a request that I buy a bottle of the very best Scotch I could get, for when her husband-to-be arrived.

After about a fortnight, Sharpless was true to his word, and a cart arrived bearing a sturdy wooden armchair with a cushioned seat, matching footstool and a delicate round pedestal table. Cio-Cio had us move these pieces around a dozen times, searching for the perfect placement in the room before she settled on a spot that would not feel a draft from the crack under the door, nor too much heat from the stove in the cooking room, and allowed him the best view out the window of the garden and his beloved ship far beyond.

We had been there for almost a month when Sharpless returned one afternoon. I had begun to be concerned that Cio-Cio had not seen or heard from Pinkerton in all this time but she seemed unfazed, reassuring me that he was such an important officer, they couldn't spare him, and that he would come as soon as he could.

She welcomed Sharpless warmly and insisted that he sit in the armchair, and put his feet up, after the long walk up the hill. Then she turned and said impatiently, "Suzuki! Why are you just standing there? Pour my guest a Scotch, then get going preparing a little meal for him! Have you completely forgotten yourself?"

I turned away to pour some of the amber liquid into a glass, hiding my flushed cheeks from her and Sharpless. I was hurt by her tone, and embarrassed by the scene she had made in front of him. I kept my head low as I placed the glass on the table beside him, but still caught the questioning look in his eyes. He too was caught off guard by her tone. I hurried into the kitchen.

As I thinly sliced tuna and placed it carefully on a bed of rice, I glanced out the tiny window and spotted the American ship, still resting at anchor in the harbour. Of course, I thought. Cio-Cio says that she is content with the absence of her future husband, but it must be gnawing at her. His ship is here still, which means he is as well, and yet he hasn't taken the time to come up to see her. He never went this long without a visit to the house when he was courting her.

So, when I rejoined them in the front room, I was relieved that Sharpless had pulled a sheet of paper from his breast pocket. I placed the small tray with the fish and rice, a little bowl of pickled ginger, and crisp seaweed on the table at his elbow. Cio-Cio was kneeling on a cushion on his other side, flushed with anticipation to hear news from Pinkerton.

"Yes, well, Pinkerton asked me to bring this note up to you, Butterfly. He regrets that he has not yet been up to see you in your new home, but..."

"Our new home, Sharpless-san." Cio-Cio corrected. "Pinkerton's and mine. This is our home where we will live together as soon as we are married."

"Yes, of course that is what I meant. So, um, he asked me to deliver this note to you." He handed her the sheet of paper with some clear relief that he felt his responsibilities had been met.

Cio-Cio looked at the writing with dismay. "Oh Sharpless-san! It is in English. Although I have been working very hard learning to speak English, I cannot yet read the language. Please, will you read it to me?"

I felt such pity for the man. The discomfort he showed as he took the note back was painful to watch.

"All right. So, he writes here, uh, 'My dearest Butterfly, my heart breaks a little each day that we are apart. My duties here on the ship have kept me hopping...'" Cio-Cio tilted her head, clearly baffled by the idea of him hopping around the ship. "No, no, he doesn't mean literally hopping. It is an American idiom. It means he is very busy. He goes on, 'I don't know if I will be able to see you at all in the upcoming weeks, but I would like us to plan for our wedding. I was thinking that the little garden at the back of the house would be a lovely place to wed. We can make it a small gathering, just a few close friends. And I have asked the chaplain here on the ship to officiate.'"

I gasped. I didn't mean to make a sound but the words rushed out. "The chaplain? A Christian wedding? But Cio-Cio, your family! They will be unhappy. And wouldn't you rather have a Buddhist ceremony?"

"Suzuki! Mind yourself! If I am to be the wife of an American officer who believes in the Christian God, then I too shall believe. I will be honoured to be married by his chaplain according to his wishes."

Sharpless looked from Cio-Cio to me and back again. He took a long sip of his Scotch, then he continued reading. "'I am thinking that the little cherry tree in the garden will be in bloom in another month. That will make a very pretty backdrop for our wedding. Shall we set the date for then, my dearest one? Sharpless here will take care of anything you need to prepare and I am sure that Junko can help you out as well. I anticipate with great pleasure the day you will become my wife, my darling Butterfly. Until I can hold you in my arms, I remain your faithful, loving beau. Benjamin Franklin Pinkerton'"

Sharpless dropped the note to his lap with a sigh. He seemed oddly deflated. In sharp contrast, Cio-Cio snatched up the note and pressed it to her chest with joy.

"A month! We are to wed in a month! Just think, the time will fly by and soon I will be Mrs. B.F. Pinkerton for the rest of my life."

It was wonderful to see her so full of happiness, but the brief expression on Sharpless' face had felt like a small pebble of concern had dropped into the pond of my soul. For the first time I felt the tiniest of doubts, and with that the thought that all that she - and I - had gone through to get to this place might have been fruitless.

The month flew by. Cio-Cio became a taskmaster of preparations. Although the house was spotless, on one clear day she had Fujio and me pull every piece of furniture, every mat and cushion from the rooms, every pot and dish from the kitchen, and all the walls, the floors, the windows, everything was scrubbed until it shone to her satisfaction. Rain or shine, I was in the garden, pulling weeds, laying stone paths and planting and pruning. Fujio went scavenging and came home with bits of lumber that he fashioned into benches and two beautiful armchairs. Fujio's handiwork was remarkable. He seemed to be able to 'see' the finished pieces in his mismatched scraps of wood. When he was done, Cio-Cio rested her hand on the back of one of the chairs where she had them placed under the little cherry tree, looking out over the harbour.

"This will be a spot for Pinkerton-san to entertain his guests on warm summer days, while he listens to his children play in the garden," she exclaimed blissfully. "And one day, Fujio, I will ask my husband to help you find a position as a carpenter's intern." The boy bowed his head low, a huge smile revealing his mouth full of charming crooked teeth.

In the evenings we bent low under the lamp light, meticulously completing the embroidery on her treasured white bridal kimono. She had me sew new soft cotton cases which she filled with two weeks' worth of sweetly scented jasmine rice for pillows for their bed.

Each day I would watch her as she laboured and, although my heart was full to see such joy on my dear friend's face, my mind would return to the shadow that I had sensed in Sharpless. I stole whatever rare unoccupied moments I could to kneel in prayer for the happy marriage Cio-Cio so desired and deserved.

I had sorely missed sharing a room with her. I missed the soft conversations thrown across the room in the darkness. So I happily agreed when, on the eve of her wedding, she asked me to sleep next to her in her bed.

"Suzuki, I am so wonderfully excited! But I fear I won't be able to sleep even a moment tonight. If I can have you next to me, perhaps it will keep me from taking wing and flying right out the window. Would you tell me a story? I will even be happy to hear one of the folk tales of your gods tonight!" And she laughed giddily.

So long into the night I whispered softly in the darkness next to her. I told her tales of wise gods and beautiful goddesses. When I ran out of the lore my grandmother had shared with me as a small child, I just made up stories, happy stories of love attained and evil conquered, of lives well-lived and glorious rebirths. When finally I felt her breathing slow and her body grow still with sleep, I glimpsed a faint glow on the horizon and gently withdrew from the warm bed to the kitchen to prepare for the wedding feast.

I heard them before I saw them. The clopping hooves of the mule and the rattle of the metal cart wheels were drowned out by the sounds of laughter and high pitched voices. The sun was barely up on what promised to be a beautiful spring day and coming up the path from town appeared Junko, sitting proudly next to the cart driver. Crowded in the back sat five of the girls from the house and Cook. Packed around them were baskets overflowing with food and flowers. I hadn't realized until I saw them all how overwhelmed I had felt, bearing all the responsibilities of this wedding day, and when I saw them it was all I could do not to cry with joy.

The driver helped Junko down then went to the back to unload the baskets. The girls jumped down, each carefully guarding their beautiful kimonos from the rough wood of the cart and the still rain-soaked ground. In a flurry of activity, the geishas gathered up the baskets and headed for my kitchen. Cook clambered down with three freshly killed and plucked chickens tied together at the necks, their heads lolling and blank eyes staring as she followed the girls. Fujio appeared at my side and I asked him and the driver to take the armloads of flowers to the garden. Once they had all vanished, Junko gently took my arm and we slowly headed to the house.

"Suzuki. Little one. How are you? I am so sorry that I haven't come up to visit you and Butterfly in your new home. The Emperor has defeated the Shogunate. The streets are safer now, without the constant confrontations between the two armies. But the Emperor has made it clear that he is far more interested in engaging in trade with foreign countries, so the harbour has been filled with ships from America, Portugal, Britain, Spain. The sailors have all heard tales of the "beautiful geishas", so the house has been so terribly busy. I have even had to hire a guard to stand at the door every evening to ensure the safety of the girls! But enough of that! What a delightful little home Pinkerton has found here! And where is our lovely bride-to-be? Shall we go to her and see what needs to be done to prepare her for her special day?"

Junko's chatter and unexpected familiarity, along with the babble of voices pouring from the kitchen, my kitchen, set my nerves on edge again. I realized that, for the past two months, other than Sharpless and the occasional delivery man, Cio-Cio, Fujio and I had been alone up here. The uproar and energy that filled the house contrasted sharply with the quiet and calm that had been our lives all this time. Then Cio-Cio emerged from her room, her excitement palpable and her joy at seeing all her friends radiating from her face, and I reminded myself that all that mattered to me was her happiness.

The hours flew by. The sun was high overhead, drying the dew from the soft pink blossoms on the cherry tree, and bearing with it the promise of warm summer days. Pinkerton and Sharpless arrived in a cart, accompanied by another much older American man. I wondered who he might be. He was not old enough to be Pinkerton's father. In contrast to Pinkerton's crisp white formal uniform, this man's uniform was a sombre black. Junko went to meet them as they stepped down from the cart, and escorted them around to the garden.

When she returned to the house, I met her at the door. "Junko-san, who is that man? Is he a friend of Pinkerton-san's?"

"He was introduced to me as a Father Hartman. Apparently he is the Christian pastor on Pinkerton's ship. He is here to officiate the ceremony."

I guess I shouldn't have been surprised. Of course Pinkerton would want a Christian wedding. But still my heart sank a little.

At last Cio-Cio was ready. She quite literally glowed. I had pinned her shiny black hair high and dressed it with silver combs and delicate white orchids. Her black eyes glittered in her white face and her lips no longer bore the bright red paint of the geisha. I glanced out the window to see the three men, whiskey in hand, standing at the back of the garden, surveying the harbour bursting with ship. Even from here I could see the flags of many countries flying in the soft breeze over the water. The geishas offered the men trays of delicate slices of radish and fresh raw tuna. Fujio had laid a path of bright flowers from the house to the men's feet. The house was filled with the mouth-watering aroma of cooking chicken, lemon and ginger.

Cio-Cio had just taken her first step into the garden. Pinkerton, still chatting animatedly about the ships, had not yet noticed her. Suddenly a commotion arose and a huge bald Japanese man dressed in vibrant orange robes appeared around the corner of the house. I was struck dumb. I don't think I had ever seen a truly obese person before. This man swayed from side to side as he walked and a dark frown filled his face. Behind him scurried several more people, some elderly women and other young men in simpler orange robes. I had never seen these people before, but recognized that the man in the lead was a Bonze.

Pinkerton and Sharpless turned at the fracas. Their eyes darted from the orange-robed man to Cio-Cio whose already white face was turning a sickly gray.

"Uncle! What are you doing here?" she exclaimed to the Bonze.

Uncle? How was it possible that in all these years she had never told me that her uncle was a revered Buddhist monk? As he approached where Cio-Cio and I stood, I bowed low, but Cio-Cio stood her ground and faced him confrontationally.

"My child. I am here to officiate your wedding, of course. When this man," pointing in the direction of the three men in the garden, "reached out to me to inform me of your plans to marry, I was naturally initially displeased that you were to wed a barbarian, but in the end I decided that at least I could give you a proper ceremony as befits a respectable Buddhist lady. Of course your aunties and these novices chose to accompany me."

Cio-Cio turned sharply to face Pinkerton, who looked as shocked as she did.

"My dear, I fear this was my doing," spoke up Sharpless, taking a few steps toward her. Perhaps I over-stepped here, but I had thought it would be pleasant for you to have some of your family here. So I did some searching and found your uncle here, and invited him to attend."

The silence that followed this announcement was broken by Pinkerton. He strode across the garden, mindless of the flowers that he was crushing underfoot. He went directly to the Bonze and held out his hand to shake.

"Well, of course! It is an honour to have you and the others join us, sir. As Butterfly's uncle, you are a most welcome guest. But you won't have to work today," he laughed. "My good friend here, Chaplain Hartman, will be officiating the ceremony."

The Bonze's eyes moved slowly from Pinkerton's face, to his outstretched hand, then to Cio-Cio. "Chaplain? A Christian chaplain? Surely, Cio-Cio, you intend to have a proper Buddhist ceremony today."

Cio-Cio bravely faced her uncle. "The man I love, the man I am marrying, is a good Christian, American man. I intend to be a dutiful wife to him. We will have a Christian ceremony and from this day forward, this will be a Christian home."

I heard the collective gasp from all the women standing behind the Bonze. Even the children, who had been racing around the garden, kicking stones from my carefully laid paths and trampling through the delicate garden beds, stopped in their tracks to gape at Cio-Cio. I looked from her defiant face, to the Bonze's reddening face, to Pinkerton. His teeth were bared in a wide grin of what could have been triumph. His expression set the butterflies to stirring in the pit of my stomach and I turned with pleading eyes to Sharpless.

Sharpless managed to step between the Bonze and Pinkerton as they faced off against each other. The Bonze paused, as if composing himself, then turned to Cio-Cio again.

"If this is your wish, then I have no choice but to excommunicate you and your household from the True Path of Buddhism and banish you from your family. You have chosen a heretical path of evil. The so-called Christian god is nothing but the machinations of these barbarians as they attempt to usurp the glorious land of the sun and our divine Emperor. Good-bye child." With that pronouncement, he waved his arm to the others still staring in shock. He whipped his robes around and stormed out of the garden, with all of Cio-Cio's family in his wake.

The silence was absolute.

"Well, my dear little Butterfly. I believe we have a marriage to enter into. Shall we? Chaplain, I believe this will be a lovely spot right here." Pinkerton took the chaplain's arm and directed him to a spot next to the cliff's edge. Sharpless contemplated Cio-Cio for a moment, then crossed over to join the men. Cio-Cio seemed a statue, staring off in the direction that her family had taken. Then Junko swept up, put her arm firmly around the girl's shoulder and led her to stand next to her husband-to-be. My feet wouldn't move. It felt like a distant memory from childhood, when, during the rainiest months, the ground around the chicken-killing stump would be so thick with mud and blood, your shoes would submerge and you would be rooted in place in the dark red goo. Excommunicated? Banished? Pinkerton's smile haunted me. The gods definitely did not seem to be smiling down on this happy day. With feet of clay and a stomach full of butterflies, I lowered my eyes and dutifully took my place behind my mistress.

Circling Butterfly

Sharpless

Sharpless

For a few months after that tumultuous wedding, things seemed pretty peaceful at the home of Pinkerton and Butterfly. I was invited once or twice a week to join him in the evening for whiskey and conversation. He had purchased a second armchair for the sitting room, but more often than not we would sit in chairs that clever Fujio had built, out in the garden, under the cherry tree. There, long hours would pass in debating America's role in the burgeoning international trade in Japan. And of course the naval conflict between America and the Philippines. That war had been dragging on for two years now, and I could see that Pinkerton was hopeful that they would deploy his ship to participate. He had been a peace-keeper for long enough and was thirsting for the blood-shed of war. As much as he enjoyed the domestic bliss and marriage bed with his young bride, he was growing restless.

After that autumn morning in 1901 when Lieutenant Pinkerton's ship, the Abraham Lincoln, sailed away from Nagasaki Harbour for the Phillippines, I made a point of dropping in regularly at Butterfly's little home on the hill. I had always appreciated her beauty, but more and more I grew to admire her steely will and remarkable skills at self-preservation. As soon as her husband left, she made it her mission to make her house as "Western" as possible, so it would welcome him when he returned. Of course, she had very little money - Pinkerton had left a small allowance for her that he asked me to dispense monthly. It was barely enough to keep food on the table and pay the meagre salaries to Suzuki and the house boy. There certainly was no money for extravagances like furniture and fine clothing. But she was determined so she got creative.

She would send Suzuki down to the market to chat with the other servants and the shopkeepers. Her mission was to determine when wealthy westerners were making plans to leave Japan and return to their homelands. This might be diplomatic staff, businessmen, military personnel. She would grill me for this information whenever she saw me as well. When she learned of an impending departure, she, Suzuki and the house boy would head out in the evening or early morning to the soon-to-be vacated home. Occasionally they would discover that, in the process of packing, the home owner had decided to leave a piece of furniture behind. They would often just deposit a chair, or side table, or cabinet in the alley behind their house.

"Sometimes it is slightly broken or scuffed," Suzuki told me, "but under Butterfly's astute eye, it has potential, and so the house boy and I silently carry it out to our trusty wagon and cart it home. The house boy makes any repairs, and perhaps I use a scrap of an old kimono to transform it into a new seat cushion." And Butterfly would proudly discard some traditional Japanese furnishing, replacing it with a piece from her husband's culture.

Slowly but surely her home began to resemble a furniture shop in Portobello Road in London. Chairs, tables, knick knacks, carpets, even landscape paintings in ornate gilt frames filled every corner of the once serene home. Whenever I would go to visit, she would proudly lead me to her husband's large leather armchair. She would prop a cushion behind my back and offer an embroidered stool for my feet. From a sideboard she would produce a cut crystal glass (with a tiny chip on the lip) and proudly pour me a generous scotch. I knew that the bottle only appeared when I arrived and I was both honoured and aghast at the amount that bottle must have cut out of her measly food budget.

The next thing Butterfly altered was her own appearance. One day I arrived to find her greeting me at the door in a tightly corseted pale blue gown, with a high ruffled collar and wide cuffs with pearl buttons. As she led me to my chair, she wobbled slightly on narrow heeled laced boots. When I went to take off my shoes, she took my arm.

"In this American home, shoes are not to be removed. We are more civilized than that!"

Again I wondered how she had managed to afford to buy such an expensive dress.

Trying not to appear obvious, I casually glanced around the room. Yet another small carpet had been spread out just inside the doors to the garden. A small burgundy stain revealed its likely reason for the previous owner's disposal. Red wine, I hoped, and not blood. Through the doors the serenity of the lovely garden seemed at odds with the chaotic room, even in the soggy winter month. The gravel paths were neatly raked. A few carefully chosen and placed larger stones brought your eye to the meticulously pruned bonsai trees. And at the back of the garden a lush wall of black bamboo masked an alleyway between the homes.

"The garden looks lovely, Butterfly. It doesn't seem to matter the season. It always seems so peaceful back there," I ventured, as tactfully as I could.

"Oh, that is Suzuki's project now," she scoffed. "I had wanted to take out the silly rocks and those tedious little trees and plant bright rose bushes and flowers that would grow red, white, and blue in honour of my adopted country that I will journey to soon, but she begged me to let her continue to care for it like this. She said it keeps her hands occupied and her mind at rest. So I agreed. She understands that once we move to America, she will have to leave that type of thing behind. Besides, life will be so wonderful and busy when we are there, she won't have to worry about her hands not having enough to do!"

The automatic gesture of her hand to her mouth as she laughed only slightly reassured me that behind all the westernized facade, Butterfly was still our beloved Cio-Cio-san. I took advantage of her mentioning Suzuki to ask, "And is Suzuki home today? I would have thought, on an unexpected sunny day, she would have been out there. Though I suppose it is still a bit chilly. And of course she probably has other chores she needs to take care of, after all…"

I could hear myself babbling and felt my cheeks redden. Butterfly's lips turned up in the tiniest of smiles and for the first time I noticed that she no longer wore the traditional bright red lipstick of the geisha. When had that happened?

"Oh Suzuki is here, Sharpless-san. Ever since I told her you had sent word that you were coming by for a visit, she has been in the kitchen preparing all your favourite dishes."

"Now, how on earth would she know what my favourite dishes are?"

Again, the little giggle escaped her lips, reminding me once more what a very young girl she still was. "It has been almost three years since we first had the great honour to meet you, my dear friend. There is much about you that we know. You would be surprised." Before my eyes the young girl became a wise woman. It was no wonder that she had captured the interest of two powerful and totally different men. She really was capable of transforming into whomever a man desired. Even I had to admit falling prey to her charms.

But then Suzuki came into the room. I felt her calm, gentle presence before I even saw her. She wore a simple, unadorned kimono, but in her hair she wore the beautiful ornament that she had once told me had been the last gift she received from her mother. She kept her eyes down-cast as she approached, and in her hands she carried a large bamboo tray laden with many delicate china bowls. The aromas of ginger and fish and sweet rice assaulted my nose and I realized that I had once again forgotten to eat anything that day. I leapt up to take the heavy tray from her.

When my fingers grazed hers, Suzuki raised her lovely black eyes to meet mine and all I could think was, "That's it, Bartie, old man. You're smitten. You're done for."

I of course knew next to nothing about love. My parents were not exactly superlative role models in this regard. To begin with, just look at the name they gave me. I have always hated my name. Really, who would want to be saddled with a moniker like Ripley Bartholomew Sharpless? You have to develop a pretty thick skin and a sharp wit to survive puberty in a New England boarding school with a name like that. Especially if you tend to the, well, portly side. You can imagine. No wonder I learned early on to talk my way out of awkward situations. Naturally I gravitated to the debating team. By junior year I was leading the team to victory over and over again. I became the golden boy of the headmaster. That spring he called me and my parents in, for a discussion about my future.

Neither of them had shown any particular interest in me once I had left the adorable stages of childhood. Mother could no longer wheel me into the salon in my glorious pram, to be cooed over by her afternoon sherry guests, only to have the nanny appear to wheel me out again before I embarrassed her by crying or spitting up on my spotless white ruffles. After about age five, Father couldn't parade me, in my oh-so-British shorts and cap, in front of his business associates who blew cigar smoke in my face and pronounced me fit to be a football full-back with my pudgy arms and legs. And, on top of all that, they insisted on calling me "Bartie".

So when, at the ripe old age of 15, the headmaster pronounced to my parents that I was a fine candidate for the legal profession, they both simultaneously turned their heads to look at me. It was as if they were seeing me for the first time. Or perhaps laying their eyes on some alien creature that had been dragged up from deep down on the ocean floor. There was a brief moment of silence before my father roared with laughter.

"A barrister! Young Bartie here? What an idea! Why, he was just home during Christmas break and I don't think he spoke more than ten words the entire time, did he, my dear?" He looked over to my mother, who smiled vaguely and waved one perfectly manicured hand randomly once before dropping it back into her lap where the other rested. "For heaven's sake, Tommy boy. Whatever would give you such an idea?" Father glanced over at Mother again for support but her glazed expression confirmed to him that she had once again lost the thread of the conversation. He looked down at me, sitting silently beside him, my hot-pink cheeks making my face look like a sausage bursting out of its white linen button-down tubing. My face grew hotter. My tie threatened to strangle me. In panic, I lifted my eyes to Head Master and caught just the tiniest of smiles and - wait! - was that a wink? I took a deep breath and turned to face my father.

"I believe I would very much like to pursue a legal profession, Father. In fact, I was even thinking that the law could lead me into politics or possibly diplomatic service. Headmaster and I have discussed this and he and I both believe I could be ready for university studies next semester, and if I continue to progress as I have, I could be ready to write the Bar in four years. I would very much like your support and your blessings." With that, I ran out of air and stared down at the tips of my shiny oxford shoes that peeked out past my rotund mid-section.

Father suggested that I take Mother to show her the display case in the entry-way, filled with trophies and banners. They dated back for decades and Father was always proud to remind me that his name figured prominently on many of the athletic awards. I tried to draw her attention to the small trophy in the corner, the Debating Club prize from Regionals. I had told her the previous month that we had won, but she had just peered at me over her cigarette in its ivory holder and her latest preferred drink, a martini. Now, as I pointed and explained once again that, see there? That gold plaque on that trophy there? There's my name right at the top. She murmured that she had left her spectacles in the car and wandered to the window to look out at the grand front lawn of the school.

But Headmaster must have said something that convinced Father, for one year later I was packed and shipped off to live at a boarding house in Cambridge. Although our home in Waltham was only an hour's carriage ride from Harvard, the parents decided that it would be better for me to have those extra two hours each day for my studies. When I argued that I could do my readings in the carriage, Father pulled me aside and said in a confidential tone, "Your mother isn't well, you know, son. I think it best she not have you crashing around under foot any longer."

With that he planted himself in his chair, put up his reading glasses, and snapped open the Boston Evening Courier.

I blurted out, "How could a boy in his room with his nose in a book possibly be 'crashing around'?"

He peered over his spectacles with a withering look. "Bartholomew. Perhaps you could save your clever rhetoric for the Harvard debating team. I am quite sure you shall excel there." And he returned to his newspaper.

The boarding house ended up being the best gift my parents could have given me. An old brownstone in the heart of Cambridge, the house was run by Mrs. Finnegan, a tiny whisper of a lady, of indeterminate years, who always seemed to wear her pearls and thick coral lipstick at every hour of day and night, and who could summon up the voice of a sergeant-major when required.

"Bartie!" she would bellow up the stairs. Even with the ever-present Gilbert and Sullivan ringing tinnily from her phonograph and my door firmly shut, that voice would startle me awake as if she were standing at the foot of the bed. "Get your hind end out of that bed, young man. The porridge is growing cold and I need to get in to clean that room of yours."

I cast a bleary eye around the spotless bedroom. The only random item, other than the stacks of books covering two small desks, was an oar. Rowan, my roommate, was on the rowing team. Rowie the Rower was of course his nickname. His bed was meticulously made. He would have been out on the water for at least an hour already, as he was most mornings.

*****

I forced myself to stay away from the little house high on the hill for several months. I sent word to Butterfly that my work had become very busy and that I would visit again as soon as I could. I was being truthful. Tensions were once again rising between the Americans and the French, both of whom had naval and trading ships at harbour here in Nagasaki. Also, because of my fluency in Japanese, I was pressed into service regularly by the British consulate to translate the endless reams of documents that were to form the Anglo-Japanese Alliance. Meanwhile the Russo-Japanese War was roiling like storm clouds on the horizon. Quiet little Nagasaki, with its unprotected harbour suddenly was feeling frighteningly vulnerable. It had survived the 1884 war with China, mostly acting as a mustering station for forces transported across the Sea of Japan to Korea. But the Russian war seemed different, bigger, more dangerous. My immediate thought was to find a way to get Suzuki to safety. And what of Butterfly? I stopped to ponder how long it had been since the last message from Pinkerton, through my office, to his wife had arrived. He had set sail in September last year. The last note I had received from him had told me that they had weathered a couple of heavy monsoons in the South China Sea and were preparing to ship out back to their home port in San Diego. That had been early in January. I had dutifully reported the news to Butterfly along with his promise that he would return soon. "When the robins build their nests," he had written.

 Winter finally gave over to the sweetness of spring. Then the heavy heat of summer was upon us. And still my diplomatic and linguistic skills were called upon again and again. I found myself spending more time in Edo, in meetings with the Emperor's people and the consuls from England and France. Occasionally I was even called upon to bear witness when envoys from Russia arrived in an attempt to negotiate over Korea and its much-desired harbours. Everyone seemed to be on edge. The Sino-Japanese War had been very costly, both in terms of resources and men lost. And now the Emperor was clearly preparing to gear up again. I wrote endless entreaties to his ministers and advisers and seemed to work night and day.

 But even in the midst of all that, every now and then something would catch my eye. I saw the first blush of pink on the cherry trees lining the wide road leading to the Palace in Edo, and thought of the sweet little cherry tree in Suzuki's garden. I glimpsed a blazing red summer sun setting over the ocean as the train brought me briefly back to Nagasaki and I remembered the bright red streak of blood on Suzuki's cut finger on the first day we met. During a moment's respite, standing outside the Consulate on an early autumn night, breathing in the cool, crisp air, I might catch sight of a lone sparkling star in the black sky and all I could think of in that moment was the same sparkle I saw in the black eyes of my beloved.

 Then I would push those thoughts aside. "Bart, old boy, you are twenty years her senior. And a member of the American diplomatic corps. It was bad enough that you were dressed down by the higher-ups for your involvement in Pinkerton's marriage."

It happened on one of my first trips to Edo after the wedding. I had been called up to act as translator in discussions between a Korean envoy and the Japanese Ministry of Foreign Affairs. It was an exhausting week. I, of course, did not speak Korean, but the Korean delegation had an interpreter who spoke Mandarin. So for each sentence, he would translate into Mandarin to me, then I would turn to the Minister and his staff and translate from there to Japanese. There were many men on both sides of the table and the stakes were high. It was essential to Japan's economy that Korea continue its trading partnership with them and not bow to China's pressure to deal exclusively with their state-run businesses. At the end of one particularly long day of negotiations, I was just preparing to return to my hotel, when an assistant to the Ambassador stopped me.

"Mr. Sharpless? Ambassador Entwhistle would like to have a word with you before you retire for the evening. Would you please join him over at the Consulate?"

As we walked the short distance along the busy Edo streets, the evening air cleared my head somewhat, but butterflies of concern mixed with the realization that I hadn't eaten in hours set my stomach on edge. Somehow I knew that a surprise, late-hour summons was not for some commendation on my fine work, but for the life of me I couldn't imagine what I might have done that would require a reprimand.

We entered the fine old home that housed the Consulate and I was immediately escorted into the Ambassador's office. Rich dark wood glowed softly in the light of a fire burning in the fireplace at one end of the room. At the other, in front of a window masked by heavy brocade curtains, a single lamp burned on a large oak desk. Although two inviting armchairs sat before the friendly fire, the Ambassador, seated behind his desk, absently waved me to a single hard chair opposite him. My mouth watered when I saw a dish of edamame and a cup of sake at his elbow, but no offer of hospitality was forthcoming, so I sat in silence and waited as he finished up with some paperwork spread across his desk. His bald head glinted in the lamplight as he bent low to read the page through his thick spectacles. Finally, he signed a document, carefully rolled a blotter over it to dry the ink, put it to one side, and looked at me for the first time.

"Sharpless, my boy. Good to see you again. I understand we are dragging you up fairly frequently from that sleepy little town of yours. All this Korea nonsense. We're grateful for your expertise. Would you like a little sake?" He indicated the carafe on the small table next to his desk.

When I politely declined, he added, "Don't blame you one bit. This wretched rice juice. Truly dreadful. The Japanese Prime Minister keeps sending me cases of the stuff. My assistant insists that I have it on hand. Diplomacy, he says. Displaying our willingness to assimilate into the Japanese culture, he says. Tastes like pig swill to me. And don't even get me started on these damned beans!" He pointed to the delicious-looking bowl of edamame sitting uneaten at his elbow.

"First let me say how much we value the work you have been doing in Nagasaki. The fact that the port there has, and continues to be, a primary entry point for American ships, both naval and commercial, is due in large part to your presence on behalf of the United States government."

I found myself blushing at the compliment. Accepting praise of any kind had never been a strong attribute.

"But... Now, son. To the business at hand. It has come to my attention that a young naval lieutenant has recently wed a Japanese girl, a geisha at that, in your town. And that you perhaps had a hand in procuring this bride for him. Is this true?"

This was not the conversation that I had been expecting. How had a quiet little wedding in a small city hundreds of miles away come to the attention of the American ambassador? And why would this event then call for a last minute summons to his office?

"Well, sir, I wouldn't say I 'procured' the young lady. Lieutenant Pinkerton, the officer in question, had met her at a social event in the, um, house where she resided. He grew very fond of her and came to me to ask about the customs and conventions of courting the girl. I, in turn, conferred with a local gentleman who was knowledgeable in these affairs and perhaps spoke a few times to the lady of the house to assure her of his honourable intentions and to query about the girl's availability to be courted."

"I see," said the Ambassador, sitting back and resting his steepled fingers under his chin.

"Is there a problem, sir? I never imagined that our government would concern itself with such a small event."

"There's the thing, son. It's not our government that is concerned. Rather the Japanese. You see, they have this fixation with keeping their race pure. You know how long they fought the concept of opening their market to us. Hell's bells! It still is an ongoing battle. I spend half my days drinking that wretched tea that tastes like watered down grass and bowing just to keep the parlay going between our countries. And it really rots their socks that they are dependent on us to help defend them against first the Chinese and now the Russkies."

He paused and looked mournfully at the cooling sake at his elbow. I made a mental note to remember to bring a bottle of whiskey as a gift the next time I was summoned to his office, though I was pretty certain that he would have nothing positive to say about the Japanese whiskey in comparison to his good American bourbon.

"So, you see, son, our position here is tenuous. It doesn't make it any better when I get a letter from the office of a…" He looked down at a letter on top of the stack of papers on his desk. "…Prince Yamadori down there in Nagasaki. It seems he believes he had a firm contract with the Madam of one of the geisha houses for this girl they call Butterfly. He feels that not only was this legal contract broken, but he lost face. And you know how these Japanese feel about being made to look foolish!"

I took a breath, preparing to explain about Pinkerton's ability to outbid the Prince for Butterfly's hand, and her desire to marry the man she loved, but he raised his hand to stop me.

"Now, I understand. The deal is done. The Prince isn't about to make a big fuss over this, I don't think. Part of the understanding in the original contract was that the girl was… shall I say, intact? Clearly that is no longer the case. No. I just want to make it plain to you that this can't happen again. I'm sure your heart was in the right place when you assisted in this alliance, but your job is consul, not matchmaker. Have I made myself clear?"

"Completely, sir. Thank you for your guidance on this subject, sir. I can assure you that this was a unique situation. If it is any consolation, the Lieutenant and his wife have taken up residence in a home quite far from the local population. They keep quite to themselves."

"Out of sight, out of mind, eh? Well, that might just be a blessing. This should all blow over pretty quickly, assuming we carry on keeping yellow and white separate, if you know what I mean."

It took all my diplomatic skills to keep my face neutral, hoping he wouldn't hear the constriction in my voice when I answered, "Yes, sir. I understand."

"Well, good then. I think that is all we need to cover. I hear you are doing fine work translating at these negotiations here. Fine work. Well, then. That will be all, Sharpless. Can you see yourself out?"

Back out in the fresh evening air, I stopped on the front steps of the Consulate and took a long, deep breath. As much as I was grateful to have escaped relatively unscathed, something deep inside of me seemed to be nagging. For the life of me, I couldn't quite make out what it might be, but figured that, being as bone-weary as I felt, it was remarkable that I could think clearly enough to find my way back to my hotel.

It took several days to settle back into the relative peace and quiet of my life in Nagasaki. My trusty young assistant, Wilson, had been fastidious about organizing the piles of paperwork that had accumulated on my desk in just those few weeks. I could deal with the priority ones on the top and whittle away at the less urgent as my energy and the number of hours in a day permitted. He had scheduled my meetings so they never fell early in the morning, late in the day or during a much-needed mid-day light meal and a solitary walk around the harbour. Still I found by the end of the day I had no energy left for anything but stripping off my stiff collar that always seemed to chafe, putting on my slippers and enjoying the fine dinner my housekeeper, Lillian had prepared. Of course, her real name wasn't Lillian. Born and raised in Nagasaki, her name was Sachi Ikeda, but she had seen a photo of the actress Lillian Gish once and from then on she insisted I call her Lillian. Strange young woman, but she was quiet, kept my house clean, took care of my laundry and always had dinner prepared for me when I got home in the evening.

Lillian. She had a special place in my heart, maybe because she reminded me somewhat of the den mother at boarding school when I was a youth. Of course, I always thought that Mrs. Carver was quite old, but looking back she must have been only in her thirties. What a job she had! Caring for her collection of hormone-driven boys. We had arrived at school from all corners of the United States, from diverse backgrounds, but all from wealthy white families, and all thinking themselves the brightest and most entitled young man in the house. By the time we all graduated and went off to our respective colleges, we had been brought down a peg or two, not least of all by our tough, loving den mother.

I chose to go to Cambridge, not because it was close to my parents' home, but because it had the most respected debating team in the country. I could have asked to return to live at home, I suppose, but Father once again made it clear to me that this was not an option, instead offering to pay for a room close to campus. So I moved into a tiny apartment in the area called Flat of the Hill, in Beacon Hill. Like most homes in the neighbourhood, there was a large flat above a shoe store. And above the flat, there was a dark little garret, barely bigger than a single room. One small window did little to give relief in the scorching summers and the winter winds passed through it as though the pane did not exist. But it was all mine! I had a hot plate, a tiny ice box, and a lavatory I shared with the large Irish family down the steep stairs.

Frankly, my Harvard years were a blur. Not being one of the footballers meant that I was invisible to all the young women over at the Annex, which was just as well. After all my years in the boys' school, girls were entirely foreign to me. I had no idea how to talk to them. Despite my great success at debating, whenever I encountered the heady aroma of a perfumed and coiffed young lady, I became utterly tongue-tied. So instead I buried myself in the library stacks and devoured everything I could find on the political and diplomatic landscape of the Asian countries.

Why Asia, you might ask? Heaven knows my mother questioned that choice each time I went home to visit my parents for a Sunday dinner. I remember sitting at my place at their large formal dining table, acres of linen tablecloth separating them across the expanse of a table for twelve, with just the three of us. Father at one end, silver carving knife in hand, slicing into the roast beef with the concentration of a surgeon. Mother, at the other end, eyes slightly out of focus, a martini in one hand, the other dropping ashes from her cigarette everywhere but into the crystal ashtray at her elbow. Me, in my childhood place halfway between them, staring at the chafing dishes of perfectly prepared scalloped potatoes and green beans, most of which would go uneaten until Cook would slip the remains into mason jars and take them home to her children. And always would come the same questions.

"Darling. Asia? Those Chinese people? They are all coming over to America, escaping that godless part of the world, barely able to survive working on that railroad they're building, or taking in laundry. It's hardly even civilized over there, you know that, don't you? My friend Mildred - you know Mildred Hawkins, from the Charity Organization Society, she held that fundraising ball last summer, remember? Well, Mildred tried to help out a young Chinese fellow who had been washing dishes at her husband's club. She hired the boy to come help her landscaper once a week. She ended up having to fire him, don't you know. She is sure he was planning to rob them blind. He was always watching them, squatting down on his heels, you know the way they do, smoking those funny little cigarettes, and peering up at them as they went about their business. And of course he never learned a bit of English. He just made her terribly uncomfortable. So she let him go. I don't blame her one bit. You just really can't trust them. So really, Bartie. Whatever would make you want to study their goings-on? They'll never amount to anything, and you certainly won't distinguish yourself in the proper diplomatic circles if your focus is over there. Isn't that right, dear?"

My father looked up from the platter of precisely sliced roast and, with a pronounced clearing of his throat, levelled his gaze on me and stated, "Your mother is right, son. I see these people hanging about every day in the city. Chinese, Mongols, and now the government is talking about starting to trade with Japan! Japan, for god's sake! Those people have been so closed off from the real world, we don't even know how backward their society is. For all we know they could be barely out of the stone age. It really makes no sense to me why we are wasting our time and resources on talking to them."

  I had tried to explain to them. I had attended a lecture given by a brilliant diplomat who was one of the first to make the journey to Japan with Commodore Perry to meet with the Emperor of Japan. He described a refined people with a cultured history that long predated our own. He talked of their deep love for the arts, their wealth of knowledge in the sciences, and the fact that they lived, on average, more than 20 years longer than we did back home. He determined that this was partly due to their diet, but also largely because they seemed to be a people with an abiding harmonious relationship amongst themselves and with their leader, the Emperor, whom they respected as one does a deity. Something in his speech touched a spot deep within me that longed for that type of peaceful, orderly life, and from that day on I strove to one day follow in his footsteps and make the voyage to the "Land of the Rising Sun".

  Eventually I gave up trying to convince my parents. I received my Baccalaureate with high honours, and went right on to studies toward my law degree. The idea of their boy becoming a barrister seemed to put their minds at rest, which meant they continued to provide the funds for my education, along with a small allowance which covered the rent of my attic home and the occasional evening out at the local drinking establishment for whiskeys and lively debates about the politics of the day. Meanwhile I also befriended a young Chinese man, the son of one of those laundry service families that my mother so disdained, and he and I scheduled weekly meetings where we would drink gallons of tea while he and I taught each other the fundamentals of our native languages. His name was Wa Wei, though he wished to be called Wayne, and by the time I had completed my law courses and passed the bar, he spoke English fluently and had landed what he saw to be a plum job as a bellhop at the tony Young's Hotel. I must admit that my Mandarin, were I to live in China, would not probably open any doors to even that mundane a career.

I articled at the prestigious law firm of Olson, Smith and Donoghue. Reginald Donoghue was an old school chum of one of my professors, who had put in a good word for me. Mr. Donoghue took me under his wing and many a night found me working late alongside him while he shared his remarkable wisdom of the future of our world. I idolized the man - it seemed to me as if he had a secret magic ball that could foresee upcoming events. And when he talked about the expansion of commerce into the countries of the East, it just inflamed my desire to know more.

I passed the bar and Mr. Donoghue immediately offered me a junior position in the firm. Although I was now in a position to begin practicing law, I really had no desire to do so. My debating skills and conflict resolution abilities would have held me in good stead in a court of law, but my dreams were loftier. But I knew I had run the course of receiving funds for schooling from my parents, so I settled in at the firm, prepared to make as good a life as I was able.

One day a note arrived for me at the office. I recognized my mother's handwriting immediately and must admit that I tossed it on my desk unopened, assuming it was a summons to the house for a Sunday dinner. It had been several weeks since I had seen them. We had gone to their favourite restaurant right after I had passed the bar. Mother had gotten into the martinis once again and she and I had the usual argument about my life. I believe this one was about finding an appropriate young woman to marry.

"Mother, I am far too busy to go off in search of a girl to court."

"Nonsense, Bartie. Several of my friends have absolutely lovely daughters of marriageable age and perfect social standing. I will make a few enquiries..."

I cut her off. "When, and if, I choose to enter into a relationship, Mother, it will be someone of my own choosing."

"One of those loose, bohemian girls from over at Radcliffe, I suppose," was her retort.

Although I barely knew a single girl from Radcliffe, I felt my anger rise on their behalf and was ready to respond in fury, when my father quietly put down his knife and fork and declared in a seething voice, "Bartholemew! If you cannot speak civilly to your Mother, this meal ends now."

I knew I had once again been put in my place and finished dinner in silence. Outside the restaurant my parents' carriage was waiting. Father asked me if I wished a ride back to my flat. Although the wind was biting cold, I politely refused, thanked him for the meal, gave Mother a cursory kiss on her cheek - trying not to take in the strong aroma of gin wafting off of her - and struck off on foot for the long trek across Boston.

That was the last time we had seen each other, so I was in no great hurry to give any attention to what was Mother's usual tactic of pretending that no harsh words had been spoken.

Her note got buried under paperwork and forgotten. I was surprised two days later when one of the clerks found me deep in the firm's library, researching precedents for an upcoming case. He informed me that there was a gentleman at the front office waiting to see me.

At first I was annoyed at the interruption. That annoyance grew to anger when I saw the man in question. It was my father's long-time butler, Mr.

Davis. At that moment I remembered the note from my mother and all I could think of was the arrogance of these people, my parents, who expect me to drop everything and answer their silly note. And when I don't, they send the servant around to embarrass me?

"Master Bartholemew, did you not receive a message from your mother?"

"Yes, Davis, I got it. But she doesn't seem to realize that I am very busy these days and can't just drop everything whenever she sends an invitation," I snapped back.

"Young sir, I am going to assume that you did not read the note?"

I prepared to bluster further but caught myself. There was something in his tone.

"Sir, your father has died. Three days ago. Your mother is beside herself. Perhaps you might consider going to see her?"

Shock, grief, embarrassment. Every emotion possible seemed to rise up in me. I don't really remember much after that. I am sure I asked Mr. Donoghue for some time off, though I am not sure. I don't know how I got to my parents' house, but I do remember walking in to find Mother in her bed, drink in hand. I remember Cook confiding in me that Mother had gone up to bed early, leaving Father in his chair by the fire, and when she came back down in the morning he was still there, his newspaper on the floor where it had fallen from his lifeless hand. Cook also said that Mother had not really eaten a bite of food since then.

I stayed on with Mother for several days. Father's younger brother George took care of all the funeral arrangements and somehow George's wife Marie and I managed to coerce Mother to get out of bed to attend the service.

A few days after the funeral I returned to my flat and my job, but tried to be as attentive to my mother's needs as I could. When, two weeks later, she still hadn't risen from her bed, I asked her doctor to pay her a visit. The next day he came to see me.

"Your mother is in an advanced state of despair. She shows marked signs of malnutrition and I fear her liver is failing due to her excessive alcohol consumption. I have run some tests but I think I can safely say that she needs to be moved into an institution for her own well-being."

So more time off was requested and I dealt with attaining power of attorney over my mother and having her moved to a sanitorium outside of the city. She didn't object much. I honestly don't think she was terribly aware of her surroundings any more. It was patently clear that she would never return to the family home, so at my Uncle George's urging, I sold the house and most of their belongings. The majority of the money went into a trust fund to ensure the payments to the institution, but I suddenly found myself with a sizeable nest egg with one parent gone and the other no longer even seeming to recognize me any longer. And in a career that would only slip farther and farther from where my true interests lay. I realized that if there was ever a time for a change, this would be it. So... I was off to England, to that other Cambridge - the famed university this time, to fully submerge myself into the studies of the history and politics of the Far East.

The Atlantic crossing seemed interminable. Looking back, I should, I suppose, be grateful for the distractions. I had booked the cheapest fare I could, with the knowledge that I was truly sailing off into the unknown and, while my inheritance was substantial, I had no idea when I might see any form of income again. The tiny cabin was well below-deck and smelled vaguely of manure from the horses being transported in the hold nearby. It was mid-July and, although it was brisk up on deck, the air below threatened to smother me. Add to that the constant creak and groan and we swayed incessantly from port to starboard, and, needless to say, I was exhausted and very relieved when we made landfall in Southampton.

I settled in nicely in Oxford. I found a small flat above a shoe shop. The tap tap tap of the cobbler's hammer and the aroma of leather, glue and oils might have bothered me were I ever home during the days, but, other than sleeping, I more or less lived on campus. I absorbed everything I could on international politics and focused my thesis on American/Japanese relations. At this point, very little diplomatic or trade communication was happening between these two countries so much of my work was almost crystal ball gazing, trying to foresee what would happen once that divide was crossed.

As luck would have it, my young Chinese friend Wayne, from back in Cambridge, had a distant cousin living near Oxford and I was able to track him down. Li Jie was a bright, spry man in his fifties who had been converted to Christianity by an Anglican missionary thirty years before and had made his way to England to live in the country of his faith. As more Chinese made the long trip in steerage around the Cape of Good Hope, he became the spiritual and paternal leader of a small, tight-knit community. He earned his living washing the floors of the Hall's Swan Brewery in Queen Street every night and devoted his weekends to proselytizing the Good Word to his fellow Chinamen.

As much as I enjoyed my Mandarin lessons from Li Jie, my real interest lay in the Land of the Rising Sun, Japan. I was growing more and more fascinated by what I read of the arts and culture of this tiny isolated nation, and the history - the stories of the Samurai, the Emperor, the wars fought to the west with China and the north with Russia - was the stuff of childhood flights of fancy. Sadly there appeared to be no Japanese community in Oxford and I feared I would never find a teacher there. I expressed this frustration in a conversation with my academic advisor, Professor

Lackey, who had been guiding me through the literature of the Orient. A few days later I received a note to pay him another visit.

"My boy," he said with puffs of pipe smoke accenting each word. It was like he was speaking in smoke signals. "Please sit. I have been giving our previous conversation a great deal of thought. I admire your initiative in wishing to expand your studies, looking beyond the walls of academia in order to fully prepare for what, I am sure, shall be a brilliant career in foreign policy with the East."

I was still so unused to praise that I felt myself blush, stared down at my shoes, and murmured a meek word of thanks.

"Nonsense, lad! Your work here has been exemplary. I have been following your progress on your American/Japanese relations with great interest. And I agree with you that your next important step is most definitely to master this most difficult language. I must admit having attempted just that a few times in my career and have never been able to get beyond the most rudimentary of greetings. So," and he paused to relight his pipe, filling the room with yet another layer of heavy smoke. "So, I have reached out to some friends in London. Bureaucratic fellows. Dreadful bores, most of them, but they do have excellent connections. Long and the short of it, I have arranged for you to meet with a Professor Alexander Williamson. Perhaps you have heard of him?"

My heart felt like it might burst out of my chest. Professor Williamson! I had been following news of him fervently, scouring newspapers for any hint of the work he was doing. The first students to come to England from Japan, a group of young men that the press had dubbed 'The Chōshū Five' had arrived in London the year before and had been placed under the guidance of the brilliant Professor Williamson at the University College London. This had been unprecedented as it demonstrated Japan's first acknowledgement that the Western world was not just a land of barbarians, but offered educational opportunities for some of their best and brightest.

"Professor Williamson, of course, has become quite fluent in Japanese in order to work with the 'Five'. He is self-taught and apparently has created an excellent program for mastering the language. If you are interested, he is willing to share this with you and meet regularly to help you along. He can also introduce you to the 'Five'. I understand they are quite a lively and humorous group of young men, once you overcome the language barrier."

We must have been quite a sight. Every Friday evening, crowded around a table at the Boar's Head. Five slim, decidedly youthful looking men, with slicked back black hair, flashing black eyes and suits of the most up-to-date British cut. They were being very generously funded by their Emperor, who had taken a personal interest in their enterprises. Squished in between them sat a stocky - dare I say portly - young American, with hair a tad too long over the collar at the back and frighteningly receding at the forehead, wearing the same coat he had through his years in Harvard. The table was awash with spilled beer from distracted pourings from the pitcher that was regularly refilled. I vainly tried to find a dry spot for my notebook where I rapidly wrote any new word I came across as the rapid-fire conversation shifted seamlessly from English to Japanese and back to English.

So that is how my year at Oxford progressed. Two days a week were spent traveling down to London, working with Professor Williamson and meeting with the Five. One afternoon I received my Mandarin lesson from Li Jie. The rest of my days were filled with completing my dissertation.

Spring finally rolled around again. Thesis completed, turned in, and defended, I started to look ahead and wonder where my road would take me next. As if on cue, I received a letter from the sanitarium where my mother had been existing but not really living all this time. The director of the facility wrote to me, sharing far more information than I would have wanted, clearly attempting to protect himself and his institution from any allegations of wrong-doing.

"Dear Master Sharpless," he wrote, "I write to you with unfortunate news. Of late your mother had become more and more delirious, often violent, to the point that, for her own safety and that of my staff, we were required to restrain her to her bed. Her doctors and I were actually in discussions as to whether a series of ice-bath treatments might lessen her distress. Then on May 20, an aide was doing her nightly rounds, checking beds. Your mother, in her agitated sleep had wound her sheet tightly around her arm and the young man feared that blood was not reaching her hand. Seeing that she appeared to be sleeping soundly, he removed the restraint on that arm to untangle her. Your mother bolted awake and swung her arm at the aide, knocking him across his face and sending him to the floor. It seems that the momentum of her arm sent her tumbling out of her bed, still restrained by one arm, and struck her throat against the night table. The aide, alarmed by the blood spurting from her neck, ran to get a nurse. By the time they returned to the room, your mother, unfortunately, had suffered too much blood loss and had passed away. We are very sorry for your loss. Please write back immediately and inform us of your wishes for her body. For the time being we have her resting in our mortuary in the cellar until we receive instructions. Again, our deepest condolences."

I tried very hard not to visualize the image of my poor mother, all alone, twisted in a sheet, hanging off a bed by one arm, bleeding out to an expanding pool on the tile floor. I prayed that her mind was so far gone, she might not have felt the pain.

This seemed a clear sign of what, at least in the short term, my plan must be. I quickly said my goodbyes to Li Jie and his family, scribbled off a hurried note to Professor Williamson, thanking him profusely and wishing the Five best of luck, and packed up my books and my few meagre belongings. Within a day, I was aboard a ship and once more crossing the Atlantic, returning to Boston.

Dear Uncle George, now well into his seventies, had once again stepped up and taken care of most of the details. Because Mother's body had been lying in the basement morgue at the sanitorium for more than a week before the director had contacted George, while simultaneously writing to me, the two men had agreed that she was a perfect candidate for the new process called cremation. By the time I disembarked from the train from New York, all that remained of Mother was a rather gaudy golden urn waiting for me on George's tiny kitchen table. Next to the urn was a small pile of correspondence addressed to my mother that George had collected from the sanatorium, and one, surprisingly, addressed to me. It was from my Cambridge advisor and mentor, Professor Lackey. In it he expressed his condolences on the passing of my mother, hoped that this letter would find its way to me, and suggested that if I were to return to Boston due to the sad circumstances perhaps I could find the time to pay him a visit in his office as he had something about which he wished to discuss. I pocketed the letter and realized that other than George and the Professor there really was no one in Boston I either needed or wanted to see. I found myself in the city that I had spent my entire youth, with no home and no parents. Having been an only child and a socially awkward one at that, there was no one here to visit. Uncle George's little flat was not at all accommodating for yet another large adult man. So I booked myself into the Parker House, a lovely new hotel on School Street.

George had placed an obituary in the Herald, including a date and time for a gathering to remember Mother. So it was, on a lovely spring afternoon, I found myself at Fera's Confectionary, Mother's favourite luncheon spot, nibbling on delicate finger sandwiches, sipping tea, and chatting with a small collection of elderly ladies who began each conversation with "Bartie! My goodness! I don't think I have seen you since you were..." followed by a gloved hand raised to about waist height. Finally I was able to extricate myself and tucked myself in a corner to smoke my pipe and observe the gathering. I watched as the older ladies, all dressed in their finest black dresses and fancy hats congregated around Uncle George, resting their gloved hands on his sleeve a tad too long and giggled perhaps rather inappropriately at some comment he whispered in their ears. And I saw George, in his elegant, if slightly dated mourning suit, his hair styled in the latest fashion, occasionally casting an wandering eye on the handsome young waiter who slid silently around the room, refilling tea cups and emptying ashtrays. I realized that there was perhaps a reason George had remained an "eligible bachelor" all these years, and likely the "black widows" orbiting his sphere were working very hard for nothing.

The day after the memorial dawned with the promise of another lovely day. I found myself restless, so after searching out a good cup of coffee - oh how I had missed those in England! - I set off for campus to meet with the Professor.

He greeted me warmly in his office and invited me to sit in one of the worn leather chairs across his disheveled desk from him. The room was filled with the aroma of his pipe, and when his secretary came in with coffee there was a chaotic moment while he attempted to gather the papers and books that littered the surface to make space for the tray. His secretary, who had been with him for decades, merely stood to one side patiently and caught my eye with a knowing smile and the tiniest of winks. When all was finally arranged, we settled in with our coffee and our pipes and, after reiterating his condolences on my loss, he sat back and insisted that I tell him everything about my time at Oxford.

As I told the tales of my adventures - the fascinating research for my paper, my lessons with Ji Lei, the trips to London to meet with Professor Williamson and the Chōshū Five - his eyes glowed and he nodded sagely from time to time. He laughed at the stories of Ji Lei trying to set up my marriage to his sister-in-law. He praised my gumption for looking outside the University for a broader education and my courage to make the journey every week to London. He asked me to say something to him in first Chinese and then Japanese, and applauded roundly when the phrases flowed easily. I believe I told him in Chinese that I threw up many times on the ocean liner to England, and was asked, along with the Five, on more than one occasion, to leave a pub for being far too loud and boisterous - in Japanese - after several pints.

Eventually my tales wound down. We chatted amiably about news about campus life and the outside world. At some point, although neither of us really noticed, the Professor's secretary returned to collect our empty coffee cups and reached around to conspicuously open the window behind him. I guess the air must have been pretty thick from hours of pipe smoke. Finally he took a moment and searched through the piles of papers on his desk until he found a document which bore an impressive government insignia.

"So, Sharpless, my boy, I hope you will excuse my impertinence. I took it upon myself, when I got word that you were returning to America, to contact a good friend who works in Foreign Affairs. He wrote back immediately, clearly very interested in the skills that you have acquired. He says," and he stopped for another moment to hunt around the desk for his spectacles, "'I would appreciate if you would let Mr.

Sharpless know that we have a position that has opened up that might be of interest to him. I understand the circumstances of his return, and send condolences on the death of his mother. Please inform him that, when his personal affairs have been completed there in Boston, I hope he can make his way to Washington to meet with me and my superiors. Our consul in Nagasaki, Japan is retiring at the end of this year and we believe Mr. Sharpless might be an excellent candidate for that position.'"

Two days later I found myself on a train bound for Washington, DC. There was a whirlwind of meetings and testing of my Japanese proficiency and training, and three weeks after that I was back on board a train, this time in a luxurious Pullman car, heading west to San Francisco. I settled onto yet another dreaded ocean liner, this time preparing for a brand new and totally unknown life in Japan. Little did I know just how new and wonderful this life would turn out to be!

Pinkerton had been gone for over two years. I continued to make the trek up the hill to Butterfly's house whenever I could. I was pleased to see that she had softened the lines of her wardrobe. She still favoured Western style dresses, but they seemed looser, less restricting, and I hoped that this was perhaps a sign of her relaxing more into a potentially long life alone in Nagasaki. The house was still chock-a-block with Western furniture. Suzuki's Buddhist altar, which had previously sat in a quiet corner of the sitting room, was now relegated to her private room.

There was only item from Butterfly's past which held pride of place on the sideboard next to the whiskey carafe. Carefully resting on a wooden stand lay a ceremonial Tantō. The blade was wrapped in a beautiful silk cloth ornately decorated with cranes. Once, in private, I asked Suzuki about the knife. She hesitantly recounted the tale of Butterfly's father. The man's father had been a well-respected Samurai. The boy was destined to follow in his footsteps, but he showed no interest and proved to be a hopeless horseman and even worse fighter. Eventually he found work as a rice merchant. He did fairly well at first, but then his sales dropped and he was forced to send several of his children away. His two sons moved to Edo as youngsters to study warcraft under their uncle. One daughter stayed at home to care for her parents as they aged. And Cio-Cio, well, you know. Cio-Cio was six years old when she was handed off to Junko. Her father never accepted that he could not protect and support his family, and one day he turned the tantō on himself and took his own life.

Most times when I visited, she would come out from her room to greet me and ask me of news from Pinkerton, and when I said I had none, she would nod sadly and excuse herself back into her room. She understood that, although I was always pleased to see her, she was not the primary focus of my visit. I was now actively courting Suzuki and she and I would sit in the garden or take a walk in the forest and talk for hours. Sometimes I would arrive with a carriage and we would go down to town to dine in one of the new restaurants that were popping up with the growth in visitors from the West. She would marvel at the choices and flavours and would giggle as she struggled to navigate the new experience of a knife and fork.

We both understood that the subject of Butterfly and Pinkerton was not discussed. She was fiercely protective of her mistress and shared nothing of her private life. And, although I think she knew as well as I did that Pinkerton was not likely to return to her, neither of us ever spoke it aloud.

Life was good. My work was satisfying. My love for Suzuki grew stronger and deeper and it was clear that the feeling was mutual. I knew that I wanted to marry her and spend my life with her, but also knew that she would not leave Butterfly as long as the young woman continued to linger in the house, marking her time till Pinkerton returned to her. That was all right. I was patient.

Another year passed. It was now three years since his ship had sailed. I was at my desk one day, drinking a tea and marvelling at how the desk had started to resemble Professor Lackey's at Cambridge. I resolved to get all the paperwork cleared before day's end, when my assistant showed up with an envelope addressed to me. I recognized the handwriting immediately and put all thoughts of straightening the desk out of my mind. I tore open the envelope and read the contents with growing heartache.

"My dear Sharpless," the letter began, "I hope this note finds you well. I apologize profusely for having been so negligent in communicating, but much has been going on in my life and I fear I have struggled with getting it all down in words.

First let me tell you that I have once again been honoured by a promotion and am now Rear Admiral Pinkerton! I am stationed permanently at the Naval Base in San Diego and am greatly enjoying the responsibilities of my new role.

I will be returning to Japan very soon. The conflict there with the Russians has become very disruptive of the trade routes for American ships and the Navy has asked me to go over to shore up our presence in the waters there. I am greatly hoping we can find a time to meet up. It has been far too long, my friend. Fleet Admiral Harley has arranged for me to command this foray and, well, he has also given permission for me to bring a... young lady along. I am looking forward to you making her acquaintance.

I met her last year at the Officers Club. Her name is Kate and she is actually the daughter of the Fleet Admiral. We are very much in love and last month I made her my wife. Now, before you become too alarmed, I met with a very knowledgeable lawyer here who looked through the contract I had with Goro and assured me that there is nothing there that legally binds me to Butterfly. And the ship's chaplain that performed the ceremony in Nagasaki very wisely (in hindsight) never got us to sign any documents at our wedding there. So I was free and clear to wed Kate. I sincerely hope that Butterfly has accepted my long absence and also moved on with her life. I realize that I should probably have written to her to inform her that she is no longer bound to me and will, of course, continue to pay for the home I purchased for her there until such time as she no longer needs me to do so. She is a lovely young woman and I expect that she will meet and marry a fine Japanese man in due course.

I will leave it to your discretion if you wish to inform Butterfly that I will be there. I fully intend to pay her a visit and explain my current situation, reassure her that her living arrangements are secure, and wish her all the best.

So, there you have it. I hope you are well and I greatly anticipate sitting down with you over a glass - or two - of scotch to hear of all your news.

With warmest regards, BF Pinkerton"

I realized I wasn't breathing. I carefully placed the letter on my desk and rested my hands on my knees, willing myself to take a deep breath. I took out my hankie and blew my nose, then took a sip of the tea that had long ago cooled. From what seemed a great distance, I was aware that my hand was shaking, threatening to spill the tepid liquid onto my lap. With great care I placed the cup back in its saucer and tried to refocus my eyes on the page that swam before me. My heart broke for poor little Butterfly. And I selfishly feared that this news could irreparably damage my relationship with Suzuki. Would she blame me?

I will confess to cowardice. I convinced myself that work was keeping me totally pre-occupied, and, to a certain extent it was. The war between Russia and

Japan showed no signs of abating. The British and the French were pushing America to take a more active part since the entire debacle was having a major impact on the movement of merchandise. China was rumbling about how its authority in the region was being undermined. And poor little Korea seemed to be hiding her head under the covers.

But none of that affected the tug at my heart whenever my mind drifted to Suzuki. Nor did it vanquish the distress caused by the burden of Pinkerton's letter.

Then there was the wave of guilt that washed over me the afternoon the Fujio, Butterfly's houseboy, arrived at my office door, hat in hand and shuffling his feet. Although he was, by this time, grown into a young man, inside this was still a shy little boy. He bowed and tugged his forelock and bowed again, murmuring apologies for disturbing such an important man, but he had been asked to deliver a note, and bowed again. When I nodded and looked at him expectantly, he stood, mouth slightly agape, for a moment then dug into the satchel he wore over his shoulder and pulled out a folded piece of paper. I couldn't help but notice the chipped and dirty fingerprints and immediately my mind went to the image of the boy and Suzuki, kneeling side-by-side next to a garden bed, discussing with great animation the ideal location to plant the latest chrysanthemum bulbs. I caught myself smiling foolishly and turned to the small candy dish I always kept on my desk. I offered it to the boy who gratefully snatched up a few treats, bowed several more times then fled my office.

The note was from Cio-Cio. In her simple elegant calligraphy, she expressed concern for my well-being and hoped that I was not working too very hard. She said that she - and Suzuki - had been missing my visits and wondered if perhaps I could join them for tea two days hence. She added mysteriously that there was something she wished to share with me, that she should have told me long ago.

Emotions flowed through me. There was a thrill of anticipation at the thought of seeing my sweet Suzuki. There was curiosity about what Cio-Cio could have to tell me. And there was deep sadness that this would have to be the time to inform her of Pinkerton's news. I wasn't sure when he would arrive back on Japanese soil, but I certainly knew that she needed to be prepared for his return and all that meant.

"Idiot," I muttered to myself. "I let Fujio leave without a reply!" I quickly scrawled an affirmative response to the invitation, grabbed my hat and ran out to the street to find a boy interested in earning a few American coins by running an errand.

The climb up the hill seemed longer and steeper than the last time and somehow we had leapt into summer with me barely having witnessed the springtime. I realized that I had spent the past several weeks, perhaps even months, trudging the short distance from home to office in the chilly pre-dawn, rarely leaving the confines of the consulate until dusk was upon us. The outside world had appeared to me to be only cold, damp and dark. It wasn't until my feet hit that familiar path that I could see how deeply my mind, body and soul had been longing for the feel of warm sunshine on my shoulders and the veritable symphony of sights and smells all around me in the forest. Despite the mildly irritating trickle of perspiration down my spine and the vague ache in my calf muscles, my step was - dare I say - jaunty and my mind turned to the anticipation of seeing my dear Suzuki. I was always so grateful for her. She seemed to hold within her a boundless well of patience and understanding. Each time I would arrive at her door, full of apologies for tardiness or a long absence, she would rest her tiny hands on my arms and smile up at me with her sweet sparkling eyes.

"Please don't, Bart-San. The work you are doing is so very important for the peace of the Japanese people. Every day you strive to make our country's relationship with the rest of the world happier and more harmonious. How could I not fully support you in whatever small way I can? I know you turn your thoughts to me from time to time. I feel in on the breeze. And you always return. I trust in that."

I quickened my pace and arrived at their door rather winded and pink-faced. Fujio greeted me in his usual abashed way and escorted me to the sitting room. As always I felt a stab of dismay when I looked around at the jumble of Western furniture, knicknacks and art that filled the room. The ever-present decanter of whiskey waited patiently on the sideboard. Aside from the odd splash offered to me, that whiskey had stood as testament all these years to Butterfly's undying commitment to her husband's return. I felt his letter burning in my breast pocket.

I turned as I heard the tap-tap of Cio-Cio's heels on the floor. She appeared in a lovely, simple gown of blue silk and smelling faintly of violets. I had a momentary thought that Suzuki might have fashioned that dress from someone's discarded kimono and marvelled at the many hours of painstaking stitching she must have put into it. Then she was settled into the chair across from me and her bright black eyes fixed on mine.

"You look tired, Sharpless-San. They make you work far too hard. But I am grateful you were able to take some time away from your important job to come visit your old friend." A small playful smile crossed her lips. "And perhaps to enjoy tea prepared by your old friend's dear companion?"

She giggled delicately at my obvious discomfiture.

"Suzuki is in the kitchen even as we speak, preparing some delectable treats for us to enjoy in the garden. But first…"

I knew what was coming next. Every time I had visited her in the last four years she had begun our conversation with the same question.

"What news do you bring me? Has the robin in America built its nest?"

I felt an enormous pang in my chest. Yes, Butterfly, I thought. The robin has most definitely built his nest. And feathered it with the finest of American beauty. And fully intends to abandon the nest he built here. I contemplated lying to the girl, ignoring the letter, and letting her continue to live in hope, but I knew that would never be fair to her, so I slowly reached into my pocket and withdrew the letter.

Her hands flew to her mouth and her eyes twinkled with tears. She tentatively reached for the note and held it folded between her hands for several minutes. When she finally unfolded it, she stared down at the ink scratches on the page, then raised it to her lips to kiss it and handed it back to me.

"Sharpless-San, please. I have worked hard to learn to speak my husband's language, but the words on the page still mystify me. Please, will you read his letter to me?"

"'My dear Sharpless,'" I began.

"Oh! See how clever he is? He knew that you and I would have remained fast friends, and that my silly brain would never learn to read American writing, so he wrote his letter specifically for you to read to me. Oh, I am sorry. Please go on."

I tried to cleared my throat but the lump there persisted.

"'My dear Sharpless,'" I repeated, and then, like a man convicted to hang from the gallows, I began to read the letter.

Her clapping hands and squeals of joy over the news of his promotion brought Suzuki from the kitchen. Her eyes locked on mine and I watched her struggle to reconcile the sorrow on my face with the elation on her mistress's. She stood rooted there as I continued on to Pinkerton's announcement that he was returning to Japan. At that moment, Butterfly jumped from her seat, spun herself around and ran to hug Suzuki.

"Do you hear? Do you? He is returning! My husband, my very, very important "Rear Admiral" husband is coming for me! And it is just as I told you, Suzuki. I know how you looked at me. I know how you doubted. But I always knew. He is coming here to get us, to bring us home with us to America, to - where did you say he is stationed?"

"San Diego," I murmured. "It is on the west coast of America in a state called California."

"We are going to live in San Diego, Suzuki! He will take us all there. You, me and Thomas!"

I saw alarm flash in Suzuki's eyes. She reached to take hold of Butterfly's arms but the girl's joy could not be contained as she danced around the room.

It took me a moment to register.

"Thomas?" I asked Suzuki. "Is she calling the houseboy Fujio 'Thomas' now?"

My beloved crossed slowly to me and rested her hand on my arm.

"Bart-San, why don't you go out to the garden? I will bring the tea out for you and Cio-Cio." She turned to face Butterfly, who had stopped in the middle of the room. Their eyes met. "I believe Cio-Cio has news that she should share with you as well.

I had barely sat down on the chair in the garden when I heard Butterfly's heels clicking on the wooden landing. I squinted into the sun that shone full into my eyes. Butterfly stood there but most of her body was hidden by a shape that wrapped itself around her neck and waist. The shape shifted and a shy face turned to face me. A long black shock of hair lay thick and shiny across the pale forehead, but it was the eyes that arrested me. As blue as cornflowers, they stared back at me inquisitively.

"Thomas," she said to the boy in her careful English, "This is Sharpless-San. He is a very special friend of your Auntie Su's and mine."

"He has funny hair," was all he said then buried his face back into Butterfly's neck.

"I am sorry, Sharpless-San. He doesn't see many people other than Suzuki, Fujio and me. And I don't think he has ever seen a person who is not Japanese."

"Thomas," I repeated, my eyes leaping from the child to Suzuki who stood erect at Butterfly's shoulder.

"Thomas is my son. He is now four years old. He is of course Pinkerton-San's child."

"But why have you kept him hidden? Why have you not told me of this before today?"

Butterfly shifted the weight of the child and took another step closer to me.

"This child is my light and my life. He has come from the love between my husband and me. But I fear that Pinkerton-San might not be pleased with bringing not just a wife, but a wife and child, back to America with him. I feared that if I told you about the boy, you would feel obliged to tell him."

A small laugh slipped from her lips. The child leaned back in her arms to smile into her face, then hid again.

"His proper name is Thomas. I named him after the famous American president, Thomas Jefferson. But here I call him Sorrow, as I fear the sorrow that his presence might cause in our lives. I look forward to the day that Pinkerton-San recognizes his own face in the boy's and I can change that name to Joy."

I had no words. Suzuki was clearly relieved to no longer have to hide Butterfly's secret from me any longer. The three of us sat in the garden, sipped tea and watched the child play happily with little blocks that Fujio had cut from scrap wood and painted in bright cheerful colours. He was a delightful boy, and I realized that I was, once again, smitten.

I had been pouring over a mountain of documents for hours. When finally I put my pen down, I felt an uncomfortable twinge in my back and rose to stretch my legs, looking out at the now so-familiar view of the Nagasaki harbour below.

"Wilson!" I bellowed into the window pane.

I heard the crash of his chair tipping over.

"Yes sir. I am right here, sir."

Without averting my eyes, I asked, "That ship. How long has that ship been here?"

The tall young man came to join me at the window and squinted through his thick spectacles.

"The American one? Oh sir! That is the Abraham Lincoln, sir. I watched it pull into the harbour yesterday morning. Did you not hear the boom of cannon fire that signalled her arrival?"

"Blast it, boy! Would I be asking if I had?"

"No sir. Of course not, sir." He stepped away and took his place in the doorway again. "Is there anything else you need, sir?"

"Damnation! Yes, a carriage, immediately. I shall be gone for the rest of the day, Wilson."

I snatched up my hat from the coat rack next to the door and brushed past him without another word. I just hoped I could get there before Butterfly and Suzuki's world came crashing down.

When I arrived back at the house, there was no sign of life. All was peaceful. The brilliant red chrysanthemums lined the path to the door. The lake of cherry blossoms that had flooded the garden in the back during the last windy day slipped around the corners of the house like bright pink rivulets. I expected that on such a sunny afternoon, both ladies would probably be in the back, Suzuki pulling up nearly invisible weeds and Butterfly sipping tea and looking out to the harbour. Looking out to the harbour! She would certainly know that the ship had arrived! I followed the cherry blossom trail where it led around the side of the house. The garden was deserted, except for three small white cushions lined up in a row at the very back, under the cherry tree. One of the cushions had been flipped over and from where I stood I could see how the fallen blossoms had stained the underside blood red.

"Bart-San! Have you brought Pinkerton with you?" Suzuki called to me from the doorway.

"No, I... He... You mean he hasn't been here yet?"

Suzuki crossed the garden and carefully placed the errant cushion back in its place.

"Cio-Cio insisted that Thomas, she and I sit in vigil all night last night. She had, of course, heard the cannons fire, and like a dog who recognizes the voice of its master, she knew without even looking that it was the Abraham Lincoln. When the entire day passed with no sign of Pinkerton, she accepted that he would have had many important duties to tend to upon arrival and would come to her as soon as he could. So we sat, back here, where she could see the ship. She waited up all night. Sometime around dawn she allowed me to put poor Thomas into his bed. I have only just convinced her to rest her eyes for a few minutes so she will look her best when her husband arrives."

Then a cascade of events occurred. Looking back it all seemed to move in slow motion. We heard a carriage pull up at the front of the house. Butterfly came out of her room and stepped out into the garden just as Pinkerton took the same path I had and rounded the side of the house. Butterfly let out the tiniest of sounds, one little 'oh' and reached her hands out to him. At that exact moment, a tall, beautiful young woman in a bright yellow gown, her blonde hair pulled up in a chignon under a matching sun hat, appeared around the corner. She paused for a moment then stepped forward and placed her hand on Pinkerton's arm. He reached up to rest his other hand on her's. At the same moment I reached down and took Suzuki's hand in mine. And for a beat we all stood exactly like that.

Then the moment was broken.

"Butterfly," said Pinkerton, taking a step forward, pulling the girl, Kate, behind him.

"No," said Cio-Cio. "Suzuki, please?" She turned stiffly, as if her body was no longer her own. Suzuki squeezed my hand once then ran to take her arm and lead her back into the house.

"What the hell, Sharpless? I thought you had explained the situation to her."

"I tried. I brought the letter to her. But... there are extenuating circumstances that... Well, I just couldn't tell her, that's all."

"Well, damn. I'm sorry, Kate, my dear. I honestly thought this would be far less troublesome. I thought you might enjoy seeing how a Japanese household is run. I thought... Well, it's all gone to hell in a handbasket now, hasn't it?"

He was facing Kate, her hands in his. She and I both spotted Butterfly when she reappeared in the doorway. This time it was Kate's turn to cry out a little "oh". Holding Butterfly's hand at her side, tiny Thomas with his jet black hair and shining blue eyes stood as erect as his four-year-old body would allow. He wore a perfect little American sailor suit and when he set those eyes on Pinkerton's back in his formal white uniform, he raised his free hand in a salute.

Pinkerton turned slowly to see what we were both staring at. For an eternity we all stood, frozen. Finally the child's spell was broken by a small voice.

"Benjamin. I feel faint."

We both hurried to Kate and took her arms, leading her to sit in one of the garden chairs. Suzuki appeared at her side with a cup of water. Meanwhile Butterfly stood still as a statue, her head held high, her hand firmly keeping the child at her side. But she needn't have worried that the boy might flee. In fact he had slightly adjusted his position to be a fraction in front of his mother. Thomas's wide blue eyes darted from face to face, taking everything in. Where I expected to see fear, I only saw curiosity and what could only be read as a fierce desire to protect his Mama-San.

"I believe I would like to go back to the ship now, Benjamin." The colour had returned to Kate's face and her jaw was locked tightly.

"Of course, my darling. The carriage is waiting for us out front. Can you walk? Here, take my arm." Pinkerton's eyes traveled from Kate to Butterfly to the boy, then settled on mine. "Sharpless. We shall talk very soon. Butterfly..." His voice trailed off as he glanced once more at the child. Then they disappeared once more around the side of the house. Kate's spine was ramrod straight and Pinkerton had the air of a deflated balloon.

As soon as we heard their horse's hooves clatter off down the hill, Butterfly scooped up the boy. Without a word, she turned her back on me and went into the house.

"You knew?" Suzuki's voice was barely a whisper.

"My dear Suzuki. Yes, it was in that letter I brought the last time. I am so sorry. I am such a coward. I just couldn't bare to tell her. She was so very happy to have received word from him. I thought I would have time to try again. I never dreamt they would just arrive at your doorstep."

A tear glistened in my sweet girl's eye. "It is all right, Bart-San. I understand. Your heart is so kind. Now I must go tend to Cio-Cio, if you will excuse me."

"Of course." She turned to leave and I found myself blurting out. "Suzuki? I love you." There. I had said it. Probably not the most opportune time, but...

Suzuki turned back to me from across the garden. "I love you as well, my Bart-San." A small smile tickled her lips then she turned and was gone.

I wasn't surprised to hear a knock on my door that night. Pinkerton's face was haggard, his bright blue eyes weary, and in his hand he held a bottle of fine American whiskey.

"I had hoped you and I would share this under happier circumstances, but I suppose this will have to do."

We settled in to chairs in the sitting room. Although it was mid-summer, the evening breeze off the ocean always brought a chill into the draughty house, so a low fire burned in the stove. We chatted for a while about mundane matters - the political situation with Russia, the British invasion into Tibet. He regaled me with details of Cy Young and his perfectly pitched game for the Boston Americans. We chatted about music. Kate had been introducing him to some modern jazz that had become so popular in California. I bemoaned the lack of good Western music in Japan and we discussed news of the latest Puccini opera that had opened to scathing reviews in Milan. I had forgotten how deeply I had missed these winding trails of conversation that came so comfortably between us.

Finally, when I paused to put another log on the fire, and he topped up our drinks, the pressing matter at hand surfaced at last.

"So, Sharpless my friend. That was quite a surprising turn of events today. It took me hours to get Kate calmed down and resting once we returned to the ship. She was definitely not pleased when I told her I was coming out to see you this evening, but then she understood that there needs to be a plan of action."

I resisted the urge to suggest that Kate's displeasure was the least of his worries, and just watched him as I relit my pipe.

"Let me begin by reassuring you that I had absolutely no idea about the child. I take full responsibility for him. Hell's bells, you just have to look at his eyes to know the boy is mine."

I nodded for him to continue.

"Once Kate was less emotional, she and I had a good, frank discussion about the situation. We agreed that clearly it is not in the best interest of the child to remain sequestered away in that lonely house on the hill. Now, to be honest, yes, my salary has increased with my new position, but Kate and I have expenses, you know. We are expected to maintain a certain standard of living. There is a great deal of entertaining involved, and events to attend, and, well, you understand that it would stretch me financially to set Butterfly up in a location more suitable for the raising of the boy. Plus we hope to have children of our own fairly soon. Not that the boy is not my own. As I said, I take responsibility for my situation here. But we need to think this all through logically, in the best interests of everyone involved."

I bit my tongue and let him carry on. It felt somewhat as if I was watching a carriage being run off a cliff, in slow motion.

"If Butterfly does not have the burden of a child, she will be free to find herself a new match. Is Goro still around? Perhaps we could enlist his help to find someone for her. A good Japanese husband, you know? I will, of course, continue to support her financially until that time. And the maid could either go with her, or I am sure Junko could help her to find a new placement, with a new mistress. Maybe they could both even go back to the geisha house again."

I feared I would crush the glass in my hand and carefully placed it on the table between us. It took all my diplomatic training to resist jumping out of my chair and going for the man's throat, but I maintained an expression of sympathy and interest.

"And the boy?" I enquired calmly.

"Well, naturally, the boy should come to live with us in America. Eventually. You can understand, old boy. Kate and I are still newlyweds. Our new home in San Diego is undergoing major renovations and decorating while we are away on this trip, and there will still be much to do when we return. And, of course, there is the matter of my position. I have only just been promoted to Rear Admiral. I am not sure how kindly the top brass will look upon me returning to base with a..."

"A bastard?" My eyes met his.

"Well, frankly, yes. There are, you know, appearances we must uphold, right? You must understand that, in your position and all."

"Appearances. Yes," I replied, holding his eyes till he broke contact to take a swig of whiskey. "So, your immediate intention when it comes to the child is...?"

"For the time being, I think it is best if things remain as they are. The child is still young. What? Three years old?"

"Thomas is four, actually," I answered.

"Right. Four. The plan is for me to conclude my business here in Nagasaki within the week. We have a couple more ports of call to make before setting off back to base. I will arrange for some extra funds to be wired to you as soon as I am home and ask that you continue to manage Butterfly's financial situation. I am certain that in two years - three tops - Kate and I will be ready and able to send for the boy. I will assure his mother that he will receive a good education and the best of care. I believe that this will be the best for all involved."

I rose slowly from my chair and stood with my back to the fire.

"The best for all involved, you say? Well, that is decent of you, old boy." I took a breath to steady myself. "Let me tell you what I think. First of all, the Maid, whose name is Suzuki, by the way, and I are very much in love. In fact, I was fully intending to ask her to marry me. A real marriage, not some brief flight of fancy. And now I find that I will need to put our future at bay for some indeterminate amount of time, as I certainly could not expect her to leave Cio-Cio-San and Thomas." I found myself spitting out their name with all the venom that I felt for this man across from me. "So, for all I wish that I could just show you the door and tell you to take your lovely bride back to America and forget about all of us and this unpleasant situation you have found yourself in, I will accept your request to continue managing Cio-Cio-San's finances, if only to in some small way hold you accountable for your situation here. Now, if you will excuse me, it is late and I feel I need to retire. And I am sure your wife is anxiously awaiting your return."

I definitely did not have any desire to go to the office the next day. If I didn't know that I had only had one glass of whiskey, I could have sworn that the heavy head and aching body were due to alcohol, but I also knew that I had spent much of the night punching my pillow and cursing into the darkness.

I had only been at my desk for about an hour when my door flew open. Fujio, red-faced and panting, braced himself against the door frame and tried to catch his breath. I was up and by his side before I was even aware that I had moved.

"Fujio! Boy! What is it? What is the matter? Is Suzuki all right? Thomas? Your mistress?"

"I... I... don't know, Sharpless-San. All I know is that I was digging in the back flower bed early this morning. You know, the spot where the water pools when it rains too hard, then all the roots begin to rot..."

"Yes, boy, yes. I know the spot. So what happened?"

"Suzuki called me into the kitchen. She seemed quite distressed. She was writing a note, and not her usual neat lettering, but all kind of scratchy and hard to read. Not that I was trying to see what she was writing in a private note, of course..."

I tried very hard to resist shaking the boy by the shoulders.

"And?"

"And then she gave me the note and told me to run with it down the hill and deliver it to you. She wouldn't even let me wash the mud from my hands."

He looked down in dismay at the dirt crusting in the cracks of his hands and the dirty fingerprints all over the paper he clutched.

I spoke as calmly as I was able to the lad.

"Give me the note, Fujio. Then get yourself a drink of water. There is a pitcher and cup on the sideboard."

The writing really was next to indecipherable. I struggled to follow the letters down the page. What became clear was that Suzuki had some grave concern about Cio-Cio's well-being and that she needed me to come right away.

"Wilson!"

This time there was no startled crash from a chair falling over.

"Yes sir. I will fetch you a carriage right away, sir."

"And, Wilson, send a messenger immediately down to the Abraham Lincoln to tell Rear Admiral Pinkerton that he needs to get up to Butterfly's house immediately!" Then as a quick afterthought, "And to leave his American wife on the ship!"

When we pulled up in front of the house, Suzuki was there waiting for us. Although he must have been heavy in her arms, she seemed to barely notice that she was clutching Thomas close to her. Sensing that something was amiss the child looked wide-eyed from me to the open doorway to Suzuki's face and back again.

I ran to them and, not even thinking of the impropriety of such a gesture, I wrapped my arms around both her and the boy. She leaned in to me for a brief moment then whispered something in Thomas's ear.

"Fujio!" she called, "Come and take Thomas to the garden. Show him where you are digging. And do not let him wander off!"

Thomas squirmed out of her arms and ran to take Fujio's hand, clearly pleased to be away from the tension that was pouring out of Suzuki like a river of energy. Once they were out of ear-shot, I caught her hand up and asked,"What is it, my dear? Why are you so concerned? Where is Cio-Cio?"

"She handed Thomas over to me yesterday after you had left. She said, 'Keep Sorrow with you tonight, Suzuki. I fear I will be too restless and I don't want to keep him awake.' She called him 'Sorrow', Bart, not 'Thomas'. I should have known how very deeply upset she was. She went into her room and closed the door. I tapped on the door in the evening to try to convince her to come out for a bite of supper, or some tea, but she didn't respond. I put Thomas to bed in my room and waited by her door all night, but she never came out and I never heard a sound, not even weeping. Finally this morning I decided to go in and check on her, but I couldn't open her door. I think she has pushed the heavy dresser in front of it. I always hated that big, dark, ugly dresser! I went to look in her window, but she has shut the blinds as well. Oh Sharpless! She is so heartbroken! All these years of waiting for the robin to build its nest in America and bring her beloved Pinkerton home to her!"

I knocked firmly on the bedroom door.

"Butterfly? Ciò-Ciò? It's Sharpless. Bart Sharpless. Can you please open the door? Suzuki is quite worried about you."

Nothing but silence. With a nod from Suzuki, I turned the knob and pushed but met immediate resistance. I glanced back at Suzuki once more, then pressed my shoulder against the door and leaned into it with my full weight. Ever so slowly the dresser scraped across the floor. How on earth did she have the strength to move it? Finally the door opened far enough that I could peer around it into the darkened room.

When my eyes adjusted, I saw that she was not in her bed, but kneeling on the tatami mat next to it, her body bent far over her knees till her head touched the floor. What came next were a series of thoughts that occurred like rain falling in individual drops in a bamboo forest.

Did she fall asleep kneeling in prayer?

I have never seen that dress before, with its pattern of white and bright red.

Wait, that is her kimono from her wedding. Did she dye it?

Have I never noticed that that tatami was pink, with deep burgundy stripes along the thread lines?

Why isn't she waking up?

What is that in her hand?

I stepped back from the doorway and looked back, past Suzuki's inquisitive face, to the sideboard. The tray with the decanter of whiskey and two glasses stood there, next to the stand where she kept her father's tantō knife. The cloth with its decoration of cranes lay on the floor below it but the knife was not there.

I took a few steps to Suzuki and laid my hands on her shoulders so she wouldn't follow my eyes to the spot where the knife should be. Behind my back I heard a loud scraping noise and realized that Fujio had slipped in behind me and pushed the door until it stood wide open. He spotted Cio-Cio and took a step back, leaving a clear view over my shoulder of the body for Suzuki.

The sound she made was like a wounded animal as she pushed past me to throw herself next to Cio-Cio. When she reached for her, the body tipped over and fell on its side. What we had seen as bloody streaks of red before became a gory, bloody mass of too many wounds to imagine. The girl had clearly stabbed the knife into her chest over and over. The metallic smell of blood hung in the air. Her hair, which she had carefully dressed up high with her favourite white flower adornment, had fallen over her open, lifeless eyes, and ugly smears of blood clung to her eyelashes and bright red lips.

Suzuki clutched her arms around herself, rocking on her knees and moaning. Behind me, I could hear Fujio vomiting helplessly where he stood. And then there was another sound, closer behind me. Right at my knee. The first word that I had heard out of the young boy's mouth.

"Mama-San?"

I just had time to reach down and pull the child's face into my leg, when one more sound cut through the horror. From far away, out the open front door and down the path, a voice, tinged with fear, and remorse, and racked with pain.

"Butterfly! Butterfly!"

Thomas/ Sorrow

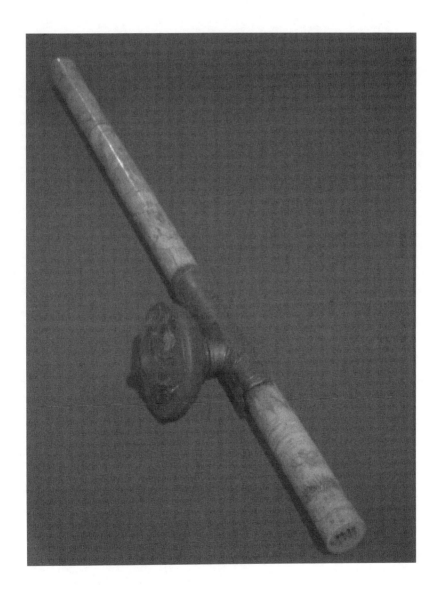

Thomas

Sometimes I dream of blood. Bright red rivers course down all around me and pool at my feet. I see it rise up until it soaks into my socks and dyes my pant hems black. And still it rises. It splashes at my knees. I try to escape it. I try to climb the hills that surround me but they are saturated with slippery blood and I can't seem to get traction, sliding back down over and over. It reaches my neck and now I can feel the acrid metallic smell burning my nostrils. When it begins to lap at my mouth, I press my lips firmly together but still it seeps in and I want to vomit from the taste. It tastes of death. It tastes of sorrow. As it rises up to fill my ears and then my nose, that is the moment I always wake up. I lie in the darkness, soaked in sweat, heart pounding, willing the dreadful images away.

I don't remember the day my Mother died. I mean, I was only four years old after all. What do you expect? I do remember waking up one night though. It must have been just days after Mama-san's death. I heard loud voices coming from the garden. I got up and looked out. Auntie Su and Uncle Bart were standing out there, and, under the full moon, I could see them as clear as day. They were standing toe-to-toe and they were having a terrible row. Uncle Bart had a piece of paper in his hand and he kept trying to show her something there and Auntie Su kept batting his hand away. I couldn't understand their words but their angry voices scared me and I slipped back under my blanket, covered my ears and sang the little lullaby Mama-san had always sung to me until I guess I fell asleep.

Many years later, I finally had a chance to ask Uncle Bart about that night. I had gone to their house during Christmas break from college. As was our tradition, that afternoon we had gone out into the woods to find and chop down a perfect pine tree to decorate. So now, we were sitting in his study. We sat in the well-worn leather chairs, our stocking feet warming on stools before the crackling fire, sharing a scotch in comfortable silence and we contemplated the flames. The room held all the smells that I have always associated with my beloved uncle - leather, whiskey, pipe tobacco and wool. The memories those scents invoked, along with the fresh wound of a big fight I had had with my girlfriend the week before, led me to break the silence.

"Uncle, I know it was a very long time ago, but do you remember an argument you and Auntie Su had in Mama-san's garden right after she died? In all these years, I don't think I have ever since heard a harsh word between you, except that one night."

Uncle Bart kept staring into the fire. I had to look over at him to see if he had even heard me. His hand unconsciously swirled the amber liquid slowly in his glass. Then he cleared his throat.

"Yes, Tom. I remember that night. I had no idea that you had heard us. We knew we needed to have that discussion so we waited until we thought you were sound asleep and went to the back of the garden to talk. But emotions ran high. I'm sorry you had to hear that."

"But what were you arguing about? There was a piece of paper. Was it something to do with me? Were you arguing about where I would go now that Mama was gone?"

"Oh no, son. Nothing to do with you. I think your Aunt and I knew right away, without either of us saying a word, that you would stay with us for as long as your Papa needed you to. No, the paper was the last legal document your Mama had asked me to prepare for her. I had no idea at the time why it was so urgent for her. I mean she was young and healthy. But she insisted that I take down her exact wishes for her internment in the event of her death. That was what Auntie Su and I were fighting over."

He slipped back into silence again. I didn't know whether I should just let it drop or ask again, but then he spoke up.

"Your Mama loved your Papa with every ounce of her being. I think she felt that way from the very day they met. Long before they married, when she and Auntie Su were living in the house up on the hill that BF had bought for her - oh and Fujio - goodness, he was just a boy then, much younger than you are now. Anyways, long before your parents married, your Mama did everything she could to adapt to a lifestyle that she thought your Papa would want. She filled the house with Western-style furniture. She insisted Suzuki learn how to prepare some American food. But the biggest thing was that she wanted to learn to become a Christian. There were plenty of Christian missionaries all over Japan at that time now that the trade barriers had been dropped. Doing their bit by saving the local heathens with the word of the Lord, I suppose." He chuckled softly and took a sip of scotch.

"So she studied with some of them. I don't know if she actually believed in God or not, but she definitely turned her back on Buddhism. That disturbed Suzuki a great deal. You know she has always been a devout believer. Su's faith has always been a bedrock in our relationship - it has seen us through many a difficult time. But this time, I had to present Su with the document, signed by Cio-Cio, spelling out her wishes for a Christian funeral and burial in the small Christian cemetery outside of town. You can imagine how she responded to that! I must admit, I guess in my own way of dealing with the grief from your mother's death, I unconsciously slipped back into the mindset of 'the Great Debater' of my youth, and stood by my professional position that this was Cio-Cio's legal document and her final wishes. Suzuki felt if her body was out in that cemetery, she could never be reborn. Yes, that was a terrible fight."

"But you resolved it, right? In the end? I actually don't remember where Mama's remains are…"

"In the end, the issue resolved of its own accord. Your mama had taken her own life, remember? No Christian church, no matter how badly they wanted converts in their flock, would allow her a final resting place in sacred grounds. Cremation was just becoming a thing in Japan at that time, so Su, your Papa and I all finally agreed to have her body cremated and we buried her ashes under her beloved cherry tree in the garden."

Those were good years, generally, even though my memories come mostly from the grainy photographs I have that commemorated the special events. I have one of Uncle Bart, Auntie Su and I in the garden at the house on the hill. We are standing under the cherry tree, which was mostly barren, as it was autumn. It was about a year and a half after Mama's death. Su is in a lovely simple kimono, Bart in his finest morning suit, and I am standing between them. I too wore a kimono with a giant bow on my head. I actually remember that kimono, because it was the colour of the sky, and Auntie Su said she loved how it matched my eyes. In the photo, I am looking straight at the camera, but Su and Bart are looking over me into each other's eyes and their love jumps right out of the image. This was their wedding day. Later when I found out about Mama's ashes, I thought it was a bit creepy that they wed standing right on the spot she was buried. But, whatever.

The three of us lived in that house, along with Fujio until he was sent off to war, for two years. Mama-san's bedroom door was firmly closed and no one stepped foot in there again during that time. My father, of course, had to return to his ship, and from there to sail back to California, with Kate, my step-mother, as always, obediently by his side. The plan was that they would return to San Diego and make arrangements for me to join them. There would have to be renovations to their brand-new home to create a bedroom for me. There were schools to look into. None of this should take much time, they said, and then we would be together in America as a family. It seemed to everyone perfectly right that I should remain in the care of Suzuki, and then her and Bart after the wedding, until I was sent for. Other than the occasional pang of missing my mother, I was by and large quite happy with the arrangement. I loved Suzuki - who quickly became Auntie Su to ensure no questions were raised concerning my orphan status by the authorities. Bart - Uncle Bart - was endlessly patient with me and would spend hours making paper boats for me to float in the pond. And Fujio, well, he was my big brother. We played catch, and we wrestled on the grass until I was breathless from giggling.

I was happy. Until one day Fujio went away. He sat me down the morning of the day he left and told me

"Sorrow (he was the only one who called me that), I have been called upon to perform an important service for our country. There is a place, across the water near China, where a great railway travels. A place called Kwantung. The evil Chinese men want to take this land away from our Emperor, and so an army of brave soldiers are going there to defend his rightful land. We are called the "Kwantung Garrison" and I am proud to be able to go and fight for Japan. But it means I have to go away for a while. I am sure it won't be for long. We are strong and brave and will fight with all the gods' blessings, and I promise I will return to you when our job is done. In the meantime, you must be a good boy for Suzuki-san and Sharpless-san. Do you promise to not be Sorrow, little Sorrow?"

I laughed at his simple joke and he taught me how to stand like a soldier and march around. I had no sense of how long he would be gone for, but he made me understood how important his responsibility to fight for our country was, and I was proud.

I certainly didn't understand when, three months later, two men in uniform arrived at the door of the house on the hill to talk to Auntie Su and Uncle Bart. I didn't understand when my aunt collapsed sobbing in my uncle's arms.

"Single shot to the head," I heard one of the men say to Uncle Bart, over the head of my aunt, as if the information had to be passed on, no matter how much pain it caused. "An honourable death, in the service of the Emperor. He had just arrived at the garrison and didn't know to keep his head low. But, by taking the shot, the artillery division was able to determine where the enemy was hiding and ferret them out. Many enemy soldiers were killed that day thanks to Fujio's unfortunate death."

Death. I understood death. It meant never coming back. Just like Mama-san. Fujio had promised me that he would come home but he had lied.

As I grew into my early formative years - seven, eight - I started seeing the pattern. Everyone lies. Mama-san had lied when she said she loved me more than anything. If she had, she would never have killed herself and left me behind. Fujio lied when he said he would come back from battle. My father had promised that he would send for me, but all I got were Christmas cards with money inside, signed "Mom and Dad". I kept the money, but tore up the cards. Uncle Bart was away a lot. The Embassy in Tokyo seemed to demand more and more of his time. Poor Auntie Su was left to cope with a young boy who was filled with rage.

One day I went out to the garden and methodically pulled up every single chrysanthemum along the path from the house to the cherry tree. I would regularly express my displeasure at the meals she so lovingly prepared for me by dumping the entire bowl onto the floor. I slammed so many doors, so often, that she took to calling me "The Terrible Mr. Bang". Somewhere deep inside I like to think that I knew I was being cruel to her, but at the time all I knew was that, like everyone else, she would probably leave me, so why should I care?

So it was no huge surprise to me when moving crates arrived at the house. For two days workmen came and went.

Back after Auntie Su and Uncle Bart had married, I vaguely remember the men arriving with a big cart, pulled by two horses. The cart had been filled with Bart's belongings, including his favourite chair and his heavy wooden bed frame. At the time I marvelled at the remarkable height of the bed as they set it up in Suzuki's room. I had never seen a bed that was anything but a pad on the floor. I wondered how I would ever climb up on it to go to sleep. But then Suzuki placed her pad on the floor in the main room and a shoji screen arrived to hide it from the rest of the room. She put my favourite of all her blankets on it and brought me over to sit with her.

"This is your room now, Thomas," she said softly. "You are becoming such a big, grown-up young man, and you deserve to have a place that is just for you."

I didn't understand why I wouldn't continue to sleep with Suzuki in the big bed that now filled her room. I had shared a bed with either her or Mama-san every night of my young life. Why were things suddenly changing? That night, after she had tucked me into my new bed, I tried to go to sleep but it all felt so strange. I tried to inhale the scent of her that lingered on the blanket, but the so-familiar bed now felt uncomfortable and, although I could hear their whispered voices in the next room, I felt very, very lonely.

"Suzuki, my love, why does he need to be in the living room? Why do we have to hide away in the bedroom all evening now, once he has gone to bed? It seems foolish to me. Won't you reconsider clearing

Cio-Cio's things out of the other bedroom and putting him in there? It's been more than a year since she... I am sure the boy has no memory of that day. I could have everything removed. I will even get Fujio to put new flooring in. We could buy all new furniture to turn it into a wonderful child's room for Thomas. Wouldn't that be better for all of us?"

"Bart-san, I cannot. I understand that this is not convenient, but please do not ask me. As long as we live in this house, I cannot bear to have that door opened again."

And so, this is how we lived. When Fujio did not return from the war, Uncle Bart tried again, this time suggesting that perhaps I could move into the tiny room in the back off the kitchen. Again Suzuki refused, and yet another door was closed, never to be reopened. Try as they might to give me a happy, loving home, it must have been difficult as I became more and more demanding and angry.

I continued to reject Suzuki's cooking, especially when she made Western style food for Bart. One day he finally lost his temper with me. He scooped me up from my cushion at the table. Bits of food was scattered all around me on the floor where I had thrown it. Without a word, he carried me to my bed and sat me down on it. I remember noticing bits of rice that had been clinging to my shirt dropped in a path through the house and onto my blanket.

"If you will not eat your Aunt's delicious dinner, then clearly you must not be hungry, so you can just go to bed."

"But it's not time for bed yet!" I declared defiantly in my high little six year old's voice.

"It is today, son. Now undress and put yourself to bed and we will talk in the morning." And he turned and returned to the table.

I sobbed and yelled until I wore myself out, then crawled, fully dressed and still with grains of rice stuck to me, under the blanket. Maybe I slept. I don't actually remember, but it was dark when I called out again.

"Auntie Su! I am hungry!"

She said nothing, but Uncle Bart answered, "I'm sorry, son. There will be no more food for you until the morning. Now go to sleep."

I hated him that night. And I hated her for not defying her husband and rescuing me.

Somehow though we carried on. They enrolled me in a school, so every morning Uncle Bart and I would take a carriage down to town. Many of the students had already been in the school for a year, so I was frustrated and embarrassed with how little I knew. Even though I complained loudly and often about how much I hated going there, hated my teacher, hated the other children, secretly I was enjoying the challenge. Again, Uncle Bart's patience came into play, as he would spend many hours reading with me, joking about how much better I was becoming at reading Japanese than him, and devising all kinds of games to help me understand my numbers. Auntie Su would bring us sweet tea and little cakes while we work and would sit sewing nearby with a tiny smile on her face. Sometimes I even forgot that I was supposed to hate them.

Until the moving men came. Somehow I had overheard nothing of their discussions about the move. In my adolescent mind, I contrived the idea that they were going to leave for one place, and I was going to be shipped off somewhere else. My anger at these horrible people who claimed to have loved me, claimed that they would care for me, and now were going to abandon me, just like everyone else, flowed out of me like molten lava from the volcanoes we were studying in science class.

I thought, "I'll show them," and wrapped a few things in my blanket. I snuck into the kitchen and took a handful of biscuits and a pear and threw them in the blanket as well. I tied it in a knot and slung it over my shoulder as I had seen some of the men down at the market carry their wares and slipped out the door, heading for the path down to town. I had never walked all the way down, but had ridden in the carriage to school for six months by this point, and the trip never seemed to take much time at all. On foot, it seemed to be miles. Occasionally I thought that perhaps I had somehow gone in the wrong direction. Things seemed unfamiliar, and around each bend of the winding path I expected to see the signs of town life - homes closer together, the path widening to become a road, the first shops that survive on the outskirts - but there was nothing but trees and the odd home that looked strange and uninviting.

Fortunately I had chosen early in the afternoon to begin my trek, so it was still light when I finally arrived in Nagasaki. It was then that I realized that I actually hadn't formulated a plan for what I would do once I got there. I considered heading to my school, but knew that it would be deserted by then. I thought about going to the docks and sneaking onto a ship bound for America, where I would find my father and he would welcome me with open arms. But what if I got on the wrong ship? Uncle Bart, Auntie Su and I had spent many a Sunday afternoon in the little park overlooking the harbour. He would point out different ships, identifying their flags, and telling me stories about the exotic countries they had sailed from. What if I ended up in Portugal by mistake? Or in enemy hands, held captive by the evil Russians? No, that would not be safe to try. But if I could get a job down on the docks, I could make a lot of money and then I could book passage on one of the ships going to America and I could travel in style to see Papa-san. Wouldn't he be proud of me then?

I sat down on the bench in the park where we had enjoyed all those Sundays and unwrapped my food. I was terribly hungry and ate all the biscuits and the pear before I thought that perhaps I should have saved some for later.

"Oh well," I said out loud to myself. "Tomorrow I will have a job and they will pay me well and I will be able to buy all the food I want."

When night fell, I found a spot in behind a bakery and tucked myself in a corner. The oven inside provided a little warmth, but I still found myself shivering from the cool night air and, I guess, from fear. I started to question my decision to run away, but reminded myself that my so-called family was about to abandon me anyways, so I just needed to stay strong and take care of myself. I unwrapped my bundle and wrapped myself up in the blanket. I curled up and made myself as small as I could. The silence surrounded me, though, in the distance I could hear the muted thudding of fishing boats nudging each other in the harbour. Occasionally there were the soft voices of young couples walking by on the street, and once a man stepped into the alley to urinate only a few feet from where I lay. I must have slept eventually since, when I opened my eyes again I could hear men's voices coming from inside the bakery, smell the wood smoke as they built up the oven's fire, and a dim morning light could be seen down the alley to the street. Before they came out and discovered me there, I gathered up my things and headed off toward the docks to get work, so I could get money then buy more food and find a place to live. It would all be easy and I would take care of myself since I clearly had no one I could trust to do it for me.

I stopped the first dock worker I could find. "Excuse me sir. Can you direct me to a boss? I am looking for work."

The man was very old, smelled terribly of fish and sweat, and when he smiled down at me I could see that he was missing most of his teeth. I stood as erect as I could and tried my best not to look intimidated by him.

"Looking for work, are you, boy? I'm guessing you want to get onto one of these big sailing ships?

Sail the seas? Go on great adventures? I am sure we can arrange that."

I hadn't thought of that. Leave Nagasaki? The thought terrified me, but at the same time gave me a thrill of excitement. That would show them! I am smart enough - the captain of the ship would realize that and then in no time I would be made a captain of my own ship. Maybe I could be a Naval officer like my father. I could go off and defeat the enemies like he does. I could be a hero!

"Yes, sir. That is what I want. Can you show me who I should talk to?"

I could see the old man hesitate. I was interrupting his work and for a moment I was sure he was going to shoo me away and tell me to go home to my mama. I stood up a little taller and did my best to look him right in the eye, like the fierce captain I would become.

Finally, his eyes softened. He looked around, maybe to see if my parents were anywhere to be seen. It was still very early in the morning. A low fog hung over the docks and, other than a handful of fishermen preparing their nets and their boats, there was no one near the water.

"All right, young man. Come with me. I think I know just the person you should talk to." He leaned over and pulled a dirty cloth bag off a pile of nets and floats. "You hungry? The wife packed me some rice and tuna. Figure I've got enough to share a little with you."

I hadn't noticed how hungry I was. When he opened a small packet and I saw the rice there, my mouth started to water and my stomach let out a loud grumble. He laughed and handed the packet to me.

"Come on. You can eat while we walk. It's not far."

He led me a short distance along the dock then veered up one street away from the water. My mouth still gummy from rice and sleep, I thought to protest that I needed to see a boss about working on the water, not in town, but then I realized that the big bosses wouldn't be down on the water. They would be in fancy offices, like Uncle Bart's, in nice modern buildings looking down on the docks. Finally he stopped at one building and held the door open for me. I walked into a large room. A man in uniform sat at a counter at the front and the rest of the room was filled with big, Western style desks and chairs. The air was thick with cigarette smoke. There seemed to be a lot of men milling around. They all turned and looked at us when we entered.

I thought, "This seems strange for a boss's office. Why is everyone in a uniform? Are they Naval uniforms? Maybe the man has brought me straight to the Japanese Navy to enlist!"

The gathering of men seemed to part like a curtain, and sitting at the back was Auntie Su. I could see that her eyes were red and her face seemed exhausted. She was perched on a wooden chair beside one of the desks and she was staring down at her hands. She looked so small and sad. I felt a maelstrom of emotions. I turned back to the old man and shot him a look of anger for his betrayal. He just shrugged his shoulders, laid his dirty hand on my head, then went back out the door. I thought of bolting out after him, but the men, the police officers, I realized, were already approaching me.

"Thomas." I heard the soft familiar voice and turned to see Auntie Su rising to her feet, her hand, clutching a hankie, at her lips.

Then she was kneeling next to me, her arms wrapped tightly around me. I felt a brief moment of comfort and relief before my eight-year-old brain kicked in again. I stiffened my body against her.

"No. Let go." I glared at the old fisherman who was now whispering to one of the officers in a corner. "You lied to me! You were never going to help me! I should have known I couldn't trust you! And you..." I turned back to Auntie Su who was sitting back on her heels, her tear-filled eyes wide, "why did you bother coming down here to find me? You don't care. You and..." I spit the name out, "Bart were just planning on handing me off to someone else anyways, right? Packing up to go who-knows-where. Well, you know what? I don't care either." The tears in my eyes were contradicting my words and, with all my strength, I broke free of her hands that still held my arms and rushed to the door. Two policemen stepped in front of me, barring my way, and I felt all the air deflate out of me.

From across the room, Su said softly, "Thomas, my sweet boy, how could you think such a thing? Uncle Bart has been searching the streets all night. When there was no sign of you, I couldn't wait at home any longer and came down here to see if there was any word. My boy, you are our whole world. And I am sorry that we haven't talked to you about the move. I guess I forget what a grown up boy you are. Yes, we are moving, all of us. Your Uncle Bart has been promoted and they want him at the Embassy in Tokyo. We thought it would be good for all of us to get out of that house and all its sad memories. Start fresh."

"But Papa-san won't be able to find me if we move!" I blurted out.

She didn't answer right away, just looked at me with sadness in her eyes.

"Of course he will find you, my little Sorrow. When your Papa is able to take you, we will always make sure he knows where you are. And in the meantime, you have a place with us, okay? Now let's go home."

For the next two days I did nothing but eat and sleep and watch workmen traipse in and out of the house. On the third day the door to my Mama-san's room opened for the first time and they coldly and unceremoniously carted everything out, onto a cart and down the hill. Uncle Bart was back at work and Auntie Su watched them silently from the kitchen doorway. I had nowhere to retreat, so curled up on my bed behind the shoji screen in the living room and covered my ears to try to drown out the sound of their shoes as they crossed in and out of that room.

That night I slipped out to behind the house where Fujio had kept all his gardening tools. I found the axe and with all my strength I chopped and chopped at the cherry tree in the garden. Auntie Su must have heard the noise because she silently came out in the darkness, took the axe from my hands, put her arm around my shoulder and led me back inside and to my bed. She never said a word to me, and I don't think she told Uncle Bart. The next morning I went out to look, expecting the tree to be practically ready to fall over. Part of me felt guilty, but mostly I hoped to see massive damage. If the tree could have bled, I would want to see a pool of blood covering the ground. Instead, there were a few chips of bark lying about and I had to peer closely at the trunk to see proof that I had been there at all.

Eventually the last of our possessions had been carted out and a carriage took us down the hill for the last time and to the train station for the long trip to Tokyo. I tried very hard to show that none of this either interested or impressed me, but I couldn't help staring out the window as what seemed like all of Japan passed us by.

There was a huge wooden house in Tokyo where I lived for four years with Uncle Bart and Auntie Su. Although our actual apartment was just a few of the upstairs rooms, I had the run of the place most days, and the Consulate staff in the offices below were - in my mind - all my playmates. The only exceptions were when I would see my aunt and uncle dressing in their finest clothes. Auntie would fuss over my uncle's tie and tug on the tails of his morning suit jacket, and she would look like a jewel in her gold embroidered kimono, with her hair pulled high and her face like a painted doll. Then I knew I was to be shut away in my bedroom with the nanny where she would read to me the stories of Tom Sawyer and Huck Finn. And Auntie always made sure that Cook put aside a plate of the delicious Japanese food she personally prepared for these events.

"April 7, 1909. Thomas, my dear boy, I am so sorry I haven't written to you in a while. My work with the Pacific Fleet has kept me very busy. I had hoped to have the opportunity to travel back to Japan to see you in your new home in Tokyo, but it just hasn't been possible. I know you are doing your very best to be a good boy for Uncle Bart and Auntie Suzuki, but I understand from letters I have received from them that you have sometimes been a little wilful and disobedient. I am counting on you, son, to be on your best behaviour. Your aunt and uncle are doing me a very big favour by taking you in and caring for you all this time. You need to be respectful and behave in the way the son of a US Rear Admiral should.

"I also wanted to share with you the excellent news that you have a baby brother. Your step-mother, Kate, gave birth to a handsome, healthy boy last month. We have named him Benjamin IV, continuing the tradition handed down from father to son since my grandfather, but we call him Benji. I look forward to you meeting him one day, and I am certain you will be a caring big brother to him.

"In the meantime, keep up with your studies, young man, and do not cause your aunt and uncle any further trouble. Your step-mother and I would enjoy receiving news from you, so please try to write to us. Uncle Bart will ensure that any letters find their way to us here in California.

"Affectionately, Father"

That afternoon I raised a ruckus by throwing rocks at the chickens in their run behind the embassy. By the time Cook came out to see what all the noise was about, one of her prized bantams lay broken and bleeding and I sat calmly on the back steps, a small pile of stones at my side. It had started innocently enough. The garden behind the house was fully fenced, with the coop and run for half a dozen chickens, a small vegetable garden, a couple of pear trees and a little koi pond. I liked to sit out there. There was a stone path that circled the pond and went from garden to kitchen door and a large flat rock next to the pond that held the warmth of the sun, even on a cool autumn day like this one. Even though Auntie Su had told me many times not to, I started tossing pebbles from the path into the pond. The ripples on the smooth surface and the flash of gold as the koi dashed for the cover of the lily pads usually calmed any chaos in my mind. This day it seemed not to be helping, so I tried aiming at the pears in the trees, using larger stones to knock the fruit from their stems. Still restless, I turned my attention to the chickens. At first there was some satisfaction in catching one on the backside with a pebble and watching it flap and squawk. Uncle Bart had told me stories of the game of baseball in America and I imagined myself growing up to be a famous pitcher like Ty Cobb. The next thing I knew I had found a nice round, baseball-sized rock, wound up like my uncle had shown me, and threw it as hard as I could at the head of the bantam. The inky black wings flew up as if in alarm but there was no sound except the crack as the rock connected with the bird's skull. Then the uproar of five panicked hens scurrying around in circles attempting to escape some unknown threat. That is what brought Cook running. The chicken lay where it had dropped, one wing still flapping and its legs futilely attempting to stand. I could see one side of its face was smashed in, the eye missing and the beak crushed. The smattering of white feathers on her chest were smeared with blood which was pooling under her into the wood chips and pebbles. I knew I should feel bad for the creature's pain but all I could feel was the void in my mind where the chaos had been.

"Thomas! Come here now!" Auntie Su's voice broke through the henhouse noise. I heard her tell Cook to get the axe to dispatch the suffering bird, then without another word she led me into the house, to my room. She pointed to my bed and when I sat on the edge of it, she turned and walked out, closing the door behind her. The room grew dark. I must have eventually slept because when the morning light woke me, I was curled up, fully dressed, with my blanket tugged up over me. The nanny came and got me, took me to the dining room for breakfast, then up to the room that had been converted to a classroom. My tutor spent the morning drilling my numbers. Lunch found me sitting across from a silent aunt who barely looked at me. I don't know if she ever told Uncle Bart about the chicken incident, but it was never spoken of.

That evening as I was being taken off to bed, Uncle Bart looked up from his newspaper, the familiar cloud of pipe smoke circling his head.

"Good night, son. Sleep well. Maybe if it is nice tomorrow, we can take a ride over to the Imperial Gardens and look at the autumn colours. Would you like that?"

I nodded enthusiastically and glanced over to Auntie Su, waiting for her to say something. She laid the mending she was working on down on her lap and reached her hand to me. When I went to her, she placed her hand on my shoulder and pulled me to her.

"I think that is a lovely idea. Some fresh air and sunshine would do us all good." She kissed my cheek. I breathed in the faint aroma of peonies that seemed to live in her shiny black hair.

"I love you, Thomas, and I know you are a good boy," she whispered in my ear.

"I love you too, Auntie Su, and I will do my best."

In 1912, at the age of 11, I was finally enrolled back in school again. My tutors at the embassy had given me a solid foundation academically but it had been two years since I had spent any time with other children and I generally found them noisy and annoying. It was a small school, run by American missionaries. Half of the students were wealthy Japanese students whose parents were preparing them for future enrolment in Harvard, Cambridge or Oxford. The other half were the children of embassy staffs. The hallways were a swirling mass of languages but the classrooms focused on English and Christianity. The teachers were busy trying to save the souls of the Japanese children, while the caucasian ones were treated like royalty. And then there was me. They had no idea how to deal with me, with my inky black hair and slightly hooded sky-blue eyes. Taking their lead from the teachers, the other students decided that I was some kind of mutant and teased me mercilessly. It was only a matter of time before I was coming home with a bloody nose or black eye.

"Thomas, my child, why do you need to fight with the other boys?"

Auntie Su sat on the edge of my bed, her eyes filled with concern and sadness. I just stared down at my bruised knuckles and thought, "Why not? They all hate me, my own father doesn't want me, and Uncle Bart has no time for me anymore."

Little did I know that Uncle Bart was knee-deep in negotiations on behalf of his government, trying to stop England and Japan from attacking China in the Siege of Tsingtau, which would be one of the precursors to WW1. All I knew was that he was rarely home for dinner, never had time to go to the park to throw a ball and barely smiled when we did happen to pass in the hallway. I just figured that he had had enough of me and would eventually convince Auntie Su to get rid of me. Even she seemed to have less time for me. When she wasn't organizing the staff for official dinners, she was off in a carriage to the Buddhist temple. Despite her high standing in the diplomatic community, she insisted on volunteering to clean the temple so at least three times a week she was down there, either praying or scrubbing. I would often come home from school at the same time as she returned from a day at the temple. Her skirt would be stained at the knees from where she had been kneeling for hours scouring the floors. There would be a smudge of dirt on her cheek and her usually perfect hair would have come loose so black tendrils would train down her back. There was a glow of satisfaction around her and I would see the Suzuki from my earliest memories from the house on the hill.

Our lives fell into a routine. I had finally established a kind of truce with the boys at school, so I came home with less bruised knuckles and black eyes. I had even formed a friendship of sorts with Robbie Harrison, the pudgy, red-headed son of the British ambassador. Like me, his parents were preoccupied with the conflict with China and the rumblings of war in Europe. Our first conversation occurred when I found him tucked around the side of the school building one afternoon during our outdoor play time. The rest of the children were involved in a game of Red Rover and I had gone off to find a hiding place. Robbie was sitting on the ground in a patch of early spring sunshine. His head was down in concentration as he sketched in a notebook, his fingers and shirt cuffs smudged black from the charcoal.

"Mind if I sit here with you? I won't disturb you. I just don't want to play that stupid game."

He looked up in surprise then nodded and waved his charcoal in the direction of a spot next to him.

"I know, right? Bloody Red Rover! Every second of our time in this bloody school has to be organized. If we're not stuck at our desks, we're playing stupid games. Not a minute the whole day to just do what we want. So I found this spot. You're welcome, just don't tell anyone else."

We sat in silence for a few moments, listening to the shrieks and laughter of the other students in the yard around the corner. Then Robbie looked at me and reached into his shirt pocket, leaving yet another black smudge. With a conspiratorial smile he pulled out a small tin box stamped "Phillip Morris".

"Want a cigarette? My father gets cases of these sent from London. They're Turkish. They're a bit harsh. I heard him talking to one of his friends the other evening and he said there are some new cigarettes coming out that are made from Egyptian tobacco that will be smoother. I'm looking forward to those."

"Does your father let you smoke them?"

"Gosh, no. But he hands these tins out like candy to his staff at the embassy so he never notices if I pilfer one occasionally. Want to try?"

I took one of the slender cigarettes. He showed me how to hold it between my thumb and fingers, how to light it, and how to inhale. I coughed so hard I thought I would throw up and he quickly peered around the corner to make sure that none of the teachers heard me. It tasted terrible. Uncle Bart had let me take the odd puff from his pipe, but you never dragged that smoke down into your lungs, and this felt horrible, but at the same time wickedly grown-up and rebellious.

We became fast friends. One day we hatched a plan. I found a jar in the kitchen at home and filled it with whiskey from Uncle Bart's decanter. The next morning we each told our drivers as we were being dropped off at the school that we were going to each other's homes after school to study. That afternoon, emboldened by the alcohol, we set off to explore Tokyo.

Much of the city had been rebuilt after the earthquake in 1855. We wandered aimlessly, stopping in a secluded corner of the Palace grounds to finish off the whiskey and smoke a cigarette.

"I know where we can go," declared Robbie. "Just the other side of city hall there is an area called Ginza. Lots of tourists go there. Whenever the younger British visitors and the sailors come by the embassy, they are always asking for directions to Ginza. I bet there will be lots of pretty young women there. Let's go see!"

A few blocks away we came into a neighbourhood of shops and restaurants. The warm spring day had brought lots of people out to wander. Rich white couples, with a black nanny trailing behind with the children, nattily dressed Japanese men with beautiful young women in the latest kimono style, street urchins and Buddhist monks all seemed to be jostling for space with the horse drawn carriages and mules pulling carts of vegetables and butchered meat in the narrow streets. The sights, sounds and smells were almost overwhelming.

Robbie grabbed my arm and tugged me down a small side street. Just in from the main road there was a shop with a dusty window displaying books and postcards. Every one showed a drawing of a beautiful, naked Japanese woman looking back provocatively at us.

"I dare you to go in," Robbie said. "I dare you to go in and swipe one of those postcards."

My eyes were locked on one picture, a card showing a young geisha. She lay on a settee, her ornate kimono draped open displaying her small perfect breasts and a dark patch of hair between her legs. Her hair was pinned high with combs of flowers and feathers and her tiny lips were painted bright red. I felt a tightening in my trousers and buttoned my jacket to mask the embarrassing hardness.

"Tell you what, we'll both go in. I will ask the shopkeeper a bunch of questions to distract him and you pocket a couple. I really like that one of the girl who looks like Mary Pickford."

We walked in, trying our best to look as mature as possible. An ancient Japanese man, smelling badly of fish and old smoke, eyed us suspiciously as we attempted to appear nonchalant, chatting too loudly in English and browsing through the books and drawings. Robbie finally approached the man, holding a book with a highly erotic cover in his hand and asked in Japanese, "Do you have a copy of this in English by any chance? I quite enjoy this author and would like to send it off to my cousin in England, but he doesn't read Japanese."

The man was momentarily flustered by this boy with the flaming red hair and bright blue eyes speaking fluent Japanese. I took my opportunity to snatch the Mary Pickford look-alike and the young geisha and slip them into my pocket.

"No? Well, perhaps another shop down the road can help me, since you clearly aren't interested in selling to the growing western market here. We shall just take our leave then. Good day, sir."

With a flourish of bravado, Robbie marched out of the store, with me in his wake. We felt the man follow us to his doorstep and watch us head back to the main street. We forced ourselves to maintain a casual pace until we cleared the corner, then took off at a run for at least three blocks. Finally we stopped, panting and laughing, and rewarded ourselves with cups of sweet tea from a shop back near city hall.

That night at dinner Uncle Bart asked, "How was your day today, Thomas?"

"Fine, I suppose," I mumbled, pushing the rice and shrimp around on my plate.

"Anything you'd like to tell us?"

"No. School was good. We had a math test. Nothing else really happened."

He waited until I stopped fidgeting and was forced to look up at him.

"You do know, I hope, that Ronald Harrison, the British Ambassador, is a good friend of mine. Right now, especially, with all the business going on in China, he and I talk pretty much daily. You can imagine our surprise today when we both happened to hear from our drivers that you and his son Robbie had made… plans today."

I felt my face turn bright red. I had a sudden panicked feeling that he knew everything - the cigarettes, the whiskey, the stealing, the naked picture hidden under my pillow. I looked over at Auntie Su then back at him. To my surprise, neither of them appeared to be angry.

"Thomas," Uncle Bart continued, "you and Robbie are thirteen years old. I understand you are wanting to explore a little freedom. It's natural. Your aunt and I trust you. I know it is a burden for you boys, but you have to remember that we and the Harrisons have a certain social and political standing here in Tokyo, so we ask that you respect that with appropriate behaviour when you are out and about. That being said, Mr. Harrison and I agreed that you both deserve to have some unstructured time, as long as, from now on, you let us know beforehand. Understood?"

"Yes sir," I stuttered. "You know, we just walked around a bit. Went to City Hall. Looked in some shop windows. Stopped for a sweet tea."

"Sounds like you had a lovely afternoon," said Auntie Su.

We all went back to our meal and nothing more was said about it. I felt like I had dodged a bullet that day, and vowed to myself to be more careful.

Robbie and I were inseparable. In the summer, to escape the heat, we went to Shinobazu Pond. We slipped around to the far end away from all the families and young couples and took off our shoes to dangle our feet in the forest of water lilies, throwing our cigarette butts and pebbles at the pink and white flowers. In autumn we took the tram out to Maple Garden, hiked deep into the forest of fiery red and yellow and climbed the tallest tree we could find. Hidden in the branches, we shared our purloined whiskey and discussed our plans for the future. We would move to New York together as soon as we were able. Robbie dreamed of becoming an artist, a famous political caricaturist like Max Beerbohm. I would write for Vanity Fair. We would get an apartment overlooking Central Park where we would hold lavish parties with lots of famous musicians and actors and would be the talk of the town. Our thirteen-year-old minds reeled at at the possibilities!

So I was surprised when, one wintry Saturday morning, we were all together at the breakfast table, and for once Uncle Bart wasn't buried in the morning newspaper.

"Thomas, I have received a letter from your father."

I slathered plum jelly on a slice of toast. "Oh? And how is the Rear Admiral Pinkerton?"

I felt Auntie Su's disapproving look, but Uncle Bart chose to ignore my sarcasm.

"He appears to be well. He says that he has been placed entirely responsible for the San Diego Naval Base, so he is not required to travel as much as he has before."

"I see. So that means that I should not expect a visit from him any time soon?" Again, Auntie Su glowered over the edge of her tea cup.

"Actually, son, what it means is that he and your stepmother have finally completed the renovations of their home, and with your father's schedule becoming much less erratic, they have decided that the time has come for you to join them."

"They want me to visit them in California?"

"No, my boy. They want you to move there. They want you to join them as a rightful member of the family."

I stared at my half-eaten toast, my mind racing as I attempted to process this information.

"Your father writes that he had been hoping that he could come to get you, but Kate, your step-mother, has just had another baby. A girl this time. They named her Lillian, after your grandmother. With Benji still in diapers and now a newborn, even with a full-time nanny living with them, your father feels it wouldn't be fair to Kate to leave her to fend for herself. So he has suggested that, you being almost fourteen now, you are responsible and mature enough to make the journey on your own."

A thousand thoughts tumbled through my mind and a thousand emotions raced through my body. I felt completely torn by the thrill of an ocean voyage, alone, to a new country. California! Maybe I could get a job writing in Hollywood! My father wants me! How can I leave Auntie Su? What about Robbie? I will be back to having no friends. Girls! Blonde girls with long legs and big breasts! I thought my mind would explode in the few seconds of silence, my toast suspended at my lips. I didn't even notice Auntie Su move, but was suddenly aware of her scent close to me. My eyes refocused and she was crouched down beside my chair. Tears were welling in her coal-black eyes. Before my teen-aged arrogance could stop me, I was clinging to her, sobbing like I hadn't cried since I was a little boy.

"Please, Auntie," I whispered through the tears, "Please don't make me go. I want to stay here with you. You are my family, not them. I promise I will be good. Just let me stay."

She gave me a quick squeeze, then gently stood up, releasing my hold. I looked up to see her and my uncle exchanging sorrowful looks over my head.

"My sweet Sorrow, you know how much I love you, but we cannot keep you here. It is your father's right to want his son and even if we wanted to deny him that right, legally we must obey. Besides, this is a wonderful opportunity for you. You get to go to America! And you will finally get to know your real family."

Uncle Bart pulled out his hankie and blew his nose, surreptitiously wiping his eyes.

"We will make sure your teacher sends you off with enough school work so you will not get behind during the crossing. I am sure your parents have already arranged an excellent school for you to attend once you arrive. Your aunt and I had discussed hosting a 'bon voyage' party for you, but I am afraid there won't be enough time to organize that, but we have invited Robbie and his parents for dinner next weekend. What with all the trouble between Japan and China right now and the likelihood of war in Europe any day, your father is very anxious to get you onto a ship and on your way as soon as possible. So we have your passage arranged for early next week."

The week flew by. The last day of school, Robbie and I met outside the building in the morning and slipped away to spend the day wandering the streets of Tokyo. Whenever the nip of the winter air would become too much, we would find a teahouse to smoke and eat sweet pastries. We vowed undying friendship no matter where we lived. We promised each other that we would fulfill our dream of living together as true bohemians in New York or Paris one day. We made a pact to write to each other every week and Robbie gave me a caricature of himself that he had drawn.

We were amazed when, seated back at our dining room table with both our families, not a word was said by any of the parents of our truancy, even though we both knew that the school would have informed them.

Then I was on the ship. Uncle Bart had given me a small tin filled with sliced ginger. He warned me that he had found the ocean voyage 'a little distressing for his tummy' and thought chewing on the ginger might help. Then he almost shyly handed me a beautiful silver flask with my name engraved on it.

"I put a spot of whiskey in there for you, since I have noticed that you have an affinity for it," he whispered.

I blushed beet red at the realization that he had probably known all along that I had been helping myself to his decanter and was infinitely grateful that it appeared he hadn't shared this knowledge with Auntie Su.

"Be safe, my boy, and know that your aunt and I are always here for you," and he shook my hand with one hand, while pulling out his hankie again with the other.

Auntie Su packed enough food for half a dozen voyages. Poor Cook must have been working day and night to prepare it all. She appeared from their room the morning of my departure wearing her most beautiful kimono, sky blue and embroidered with hundreds of intricate butterflies. Her hair was pulled up high and held in place with her most delicate ornament, the one she had told me once was the only thing she had left from her own mother.

"I have one last thing for you to pack away into your trunk, Thomas," she said. She handed me a long object wrapped in a slightly worn, red velvet cloth. Inside the cloth was a beautiful ceremonial dagger. The silver blade curved slightly inward and the ivory handle was ornately carved.

"You probably don't remember this tanto. It has been packed away since, well, since you were very little. Although it is tinged with a great deal of sadness, it did belong to your mother, and to her father before that, and, like my hair ornament, it is the only thing that I can give you that comes from her. I trust you to guard it well and one day, when you have your own home, you can display it as a proud reminder of your samurai heritage."

Two days out at sea, I was invited to dine at the captain's table. I assumed it was my uncle's diplomatic status that had earned me the honour. He had, after all, used his influence to acquire quite a top-notch cabin on the ship. It didn't take me long after I had been seated at the table, surrounded by elegant gentlemen in morning suits and elderly ladies dripping in jewels, to understand that my father was, in fact, the cause of my celebrity status.

"I hear you are Admiral Pinkerton's son," drawled the woman to my left. She looked ancient. Her grey hair was pulled back in a severe bun, and sitting so close I could see her face powder collecting in the million creases in her face. She smelled overwhelmingly of roses and, as I begrudgingly sipped the water in my glass, I calculated how many bottles of fine whiskey I could buy with just one of the diamonds sparkling at her ears and wrist.

"Yes, ma'am."

"Well, my Lord, boy! What is God's green earth were you doing way off in that godforsaken country all by yourself?" bellowed the southern man across from me. It took me a moment to understand his accent. I had never come across a drawl like his and none of his words sounded like any English I had ever heard.

"I have been living with my aunt and uncle in Tokyo, sir. I am actually just coming to America for the first time. My uncle, Ambassador Sharpless, and his wife, Suzuki, have been raising me." I emphasized her Japanese name in the hope that he wouldn't say anything else derogatory about the country that I now felt very protective of.

"Well, shoot! How about that? I met the ambassador at a trade function just last week. I had no idea he had married one of them."

It took every ounce of control to avoid lashing out at him and the others who sat around me, nodding and whispering this scandalous news down the length of the table. Only my desire not to embarrass my aunt and uncle kept me silently steaming as I toyed with the roast beef on my plate and quietly longed for a cigarette and a drink. Little did I know that this was just a taste of what was to be in my future.

Fortunately it didn't take me long to discover that most of the workers on board were Japanese or Chinese. Using my broken Mandarin that I had been forced to learn from Uncle Bart, I befriended a young busboy in the dining room named Cho and he became adept at sneaking out nearly empty liquor bottles from the bar and could charm handfuls of cigarettes from the hostesses who offered them to the passengers. Late at night, after his workday was finally over, we would meet on deck, hidden behind a lifeboat and drink whatever he had acquired that day. He would have been fired if he had been caught on the passenger deck, even if legitimately invited. We would talk long into the night, watching the wide-open star-filled sky. It was probably fortunate that we had young, strong constitutions and weren't poisoned by the combination of wine, whiskey, gin, sherry, port and whatever other alcohol he had procured that day, But he certainly made the journey endurable, compared to the endless hours above deck with bejewelled matriarchs and cigar-puffing wind-bags. There were a few young women on board. I would see them across the dining room at dinner, fair-haired beauties with flawless skin and elegant gowns that exposed the ivory perfection of the tops of their bosoms. I, of course, had seen photos of such girls. Buried deep in my trunk, stowed away for the voyage, was my collection of postcards from my days of wandering the Tokyo streets with Robbie. Coloured photos of brassy blondes with bare breasts, red lips and inviting eyes. But these girls, here at dinner, who flashed me small, coy smiles with downturned eyes, were kept on very tight leashes by their mothers who stared openly at my strange combination of black hair and blue eyes under hooded lids. Dinner became a nightly saga of unrequited lust that I judiciously hid beneath the napkin on my lap.

But at night, in the darkness with Cho, we shared our stories and our dreams. I confessed my fears of leaving behind my family and my friend to move to a strange land. We revealed that we had both lost our parents at a young age. His mother, father and sister had all been killed in the Xinhai Revolution. His father had been loyal to the Imperial dynasty and, when it was overthrown, soldiers had come to their home in Beijing and murdered them all. Cho had been spared because he was staying with his aunt and uncle in the country but the entire family feared the retribution of the Republican forces and chose to flee. They had stowed away in a freighter to America, a hellish voyage below decks in the stables in cargo holds, hiding in the straw and eating the horses' oats to survive. One of the hands caring for the horses down there had discovered them and kept their secret and, upon docking in San Francisco, had even managed to secure Cho a job with him. So for two years Cho repeated the voyage many times, still in the hold, shovelling manure and working hard before he was able to apply for and receive a promotion to the position of busboy. He had grown to love the open seas and was content, despite the long days and the often brutal treatment of the passengers toward the "chinamen" doing their bidding.

Cho's aunt, uncle and cousins had made it safely to shore and, through the support of their new-found community of Chinese immigrants in San Francisco were able to find a small apartment to rent. His uncle got work in the laundry room of the recently built Hotel Montgomery. Before we docked in San Diego Cho gave me a piece of paper with his family's names and addresses in San Francisco. He missed them terribly and asked, if I ever got the chance, to go to see them and send them his love.

The first thing I noticed as I walked down the gangplank in San Diego was the smell. After the fresh, clean air of the open seas, I was hit with an avalanche of aromas - fish, the fumes from what appeared to be thousands of automobiles and what seemed to be the unwashed smell of far too many men working on the docks. They pushed and jostled me when I stopped to get my bearings. The ship's valet waited patiently behind me, smoking a cigarette, leaning on my trunk, and clearly in no hurry to return to the boat to collect more luggage.

"You have people coming to meet you, young Sir?" he shouted over the noise of voices, carts and vehicles.

"Yes. At least I thought so," I answered, craning my neck over the crowd for some sign of my father.

At last, when most of the passengers had cleared the causeway, I spotted a young man in naval uniform, standing rigidly at attention, holding a sign that said 'Thomas Pinkerton'. I headed in his direction and, with a sigh, the valet stubbed out his cigarette and followed on my heels.

"Master Pinkerton?" the young officer asked.

"Yes, that's me. Is my father here?"

"I'm afraid your father was not able to meet you. He asked me to come and deliver you to his home. I believe Mrs. Pinkerton is expecting you there. Right this way. I have a car and driver waiting for us."

The home was spectacular. Situated on a rolling hill on the outskirt of the city, it had a beautiful view across a vast field entirely of grass, looking out to the ocean. The house seemed palatial. I had never seen a private home this size, set in what appeared to be a park. As we pulled up to the front entrance a man in very formal dress opened the door and stood waiting for me to get out of the car and approach him.

"Master Thomas, I assume? I am Mr. Lawrence, Admiral Pinkerton's butler. Welcome to your new home. Please come in."

I looked back to the car, prepared to fetch my luggage.

"Don't you worry about your belongings. These gentlemen," nodding toward the young officer and the driver, "will ensure they all get placed in your room. Right this way. I am afraid the Mistress is indisposed at the moment, but I am certain she will be available to greet you herself shortly."

And so I found myself, sitting gingerly on a spotless white bed in a sterile white bedroom surrounded by the trunk and luggage that Uncle Bart had purchased for the trip, thinking nervously about the marks they and my shoes might be leaving on the thick white carpet. I peeked under the bed in search of a chamber pot. When I couldn't hold it in any longer, I ventured out into the hallway, thinking I could perhaps slip unnoticed outside and find a private place to relieve myself.

"Thomas!" I heard from the bottom of the stairs. "Is it really you? My, how big you've grown! I do hope God granted you an easy crossing. I personally hate ocean travel, but of course your father loves it. Do come down here. We must have coffee. Are you ravenous? Of course you are. I will get Cook to prepare us a snack."

I stood frozen on the top step as this cascade of words flowed over me. All I could think about was that now I wasn't going to be able to pee. The sun through the high windows of the entryway blinded me but I could make out the shape of what I assumed was my stepmother. I descended the wide staircase, each step another pillow of white carpeting, until I came face-to-face with the woman who was to become my mother.

She stood serenely next to a table with a giant floral arrangement of white lilies in a tall, blood red ceramic vase. A matching lily was pinned into her shiny blonde hair. She would have appeared angelic were it not for the tense smile that almost obscured her lips and did not reach her eyes. I felt immediately unwanted in her presence.

"Thank you... um..." I stumbled.

"Please. You must call me Mama. That is what the children call me. And of course your father is Papa."

My heart sank. I didn't know how to tell her that my mother, my real mother, was Mama. Although I could barely remember her, Auntie Su had always called her that when she told me stories of their life together. Cio-Cio-san was Mama, not this woman standing before me, emanating vaguely veiled hostility.

"Thank you..." She tilted her head in anticipation. "... Mama. Would it be possible for me to, um, freshen up?"

"Why of course! Lawrence?"

The butler appeared immediately from a side room, as if he had been standing just the other side of the door.

"Show Thomas to the powder room," she ordered. "Then, Thomas, please join me in the sunroom and we can get to know each other a little before Papa comes home."

Fearing that Mr. Lawrence wasn't hovering outside the washroom door, I stifled the sigh of gratitude when I finally relieved myself. It took me a few minutes to figure out how the toilet flushed. The embassy in Tokyo had only recently retrofitted an indoor facility and it did not operate using a chain dangling over your head.

"Perhaps you should make a pot of tea, Mildred. You know how these oriental types love their tea," I heard from the back of the house.

I followed her voice till I came upon a room with so many windows the sun seemed to be everywhere. Kate was sitting on a wicker settee with a cup in her hand. On the table next to her was a lamp with crystal prisms dangling from it and the light created rainbows of colour to dance on all the surfaces. I felt momentarily dizzy.

"Come, Thomas. Sit here across from me. Coffee? Or do you prefer tea?"

I had just settled into the wicker chair opposite her when a young woman appeared at the door.

"Ma'am? It's Lillian. She is up from her nap and I'm afraid she is quite fussy."

"Oh, that girl! She is always crying about something. Not like her brother, Benji. What a sweet boy he is, always has been. But Lillian? I swear if I didn't have Camille here, I wouldn't ever get anything done. Won't you excuse me, Thomas? Please relax here, have your coffee. Or tea, of course, if you'd rather. There is some lovely shortbread here. Cook knows how much I love my sweets! I am sure Papa will be home shortly and Benji will be down from his lessons, then we can sit down for supper together and you can tell us all about what you have been up to all these years."

With that, she swept out of the room. I picked up the cup of dark brown liquid. Of course I had heard of coffee, but Uncle Bart and Auntie Su had never had it in our home and it had never occurred to me to try it. I took a sip and immediately spit it back into the cup. I had never tasted anything so bitter in my life! I noticed the little bowl of sugar and the pitcher of milk next to the coffee pot on a tray and realized that must be how they make it drinkable. I shovelled three large spoonfuls of sugar into my cup and filled it to the rim with milk. When I tasted it again, it still seemed unpleasant, and certainly didn't seem to do anything to cut my thirst, but I assumed this was my first lesson in learning how to become an American, so I picked up a cookie - a shortbread she had called it - and sat back to wait.

Dinner was a formal affair, but, as I was soon to discover, dinner was always a formal affair. Benji and Lillian were trotted out to meet me. They were both very pretty children, very fair, with blue eyes I recognized from my own reflection in the mirror. They seemed sincerely terrified of me, hiding behind Camille's skirt and unwilling to shake hands no matter how hard their parents tried. Finally they were allowed to retreat to the kitchen where they would eat their supper with the servants and I was left to face my father for the first time.

He seemed enormous. He wore his black naval uniform and the buttons shone in the candlelight. He sat very erect, with a glass of whiskey and a cigarette burning in an ashtray at his elbow.

"Benjamin, dear, put out that cigarette, please. Cook is about to bring out dinner. Let's say Grace."

He did what he was told, then they both bowed their heads. Papa mumbled something indiscernible then they both said, "Amen". Whatever that was, it was apparently 'Grace'. As if on cue, Cook, a woman as wide as she was tall, with a little ruffled bonnet on her head and a pristine white apron covering her girth, arrived with plates piled high with food. Lawrence followed behind with a third plate. Not another word was spoken until Papa's plate was finished. Cook magically reappeared and took all three plates away, even though I certainly felt like I could have eaten more, and Kate seemed to have barely touched her's.

"Cook, another excellent feast, as always!" said Papa.

"Thank you, sir. Glad you liked it, sir," said Cook as she pushed through the swinging door into the kitchen.

"Well, Thomas, my boy, you must be exhausted after your long trip. What say you we leave off our conversation till tomorrow, shall we? I have a stack of paperwork I need to tend to this evening," and he rose, took up his whiskey, and vanished from the room.

We never did actually have that conversation. What we did end up having instead was regular bible readings. Most evenings when we were all at home, after dinner we would adjourn to the formal sitting room. It appeared that the sunroom was Kate's domain as I never once saw Papa go in there. Papa and Kate would sit in matching armchairs facing a lectern which held a massive bible. It would be open to a specific passage for that day's study. The children would be led in. Lillian would climb up onto her mother's lap from where she stared at me with the sort of curiosity one would normally reserve for animals in a zoo. Benji would solemnly push over a low stool to in front of the lectern and climb onto it so he could see the page, then slowly and methodically he would read the passage chosen. Just as my eyes would be beginning to glaze over I would hear, "Excellent work, Benji. Thank you. Now, Thomas, your turn."

Benji would grin from ear to ear from his father's praise then plop down at his feet and turn those same unnerving eyes to me. I had been reading in English most of my life, but these words seemed stilted and foreign and I would stumble through to the end of the passage.

"Better, Thomas." Kate would usually say. "You could learn from Benji here and take a little more time and care with your reading. These are sacred words that Our Lord has honoured us with and I am sure you understand what a gift we have been given. Now, children, off you go. Wash up, say your prayers and I will be up to tuck you in."

With that, I seemed to also be dismissed. I soon found myself slipping out every night to a bench under a low hanging willow tree where I kept a secret stash of Papa's whiskey and cigarettes. It wasn't a horrible life, but it certainly was a boring one, and I missed my friend Robbie, Uncle Bart and Auntie Su terribly.

Eventually, one evening at dinner I screwed up my courage. "Papa?"

He seemed startled to have been spoken to during the meal.

"I was wondering if I could possibly come down into the city with you tomorrow? I have yet to actually see San Diego and I hear that" and here I found a moment of divine inspiration, "there are some lovely churches to see." I smiled my most winning smile at them each in turn.

I saw the tiniest of nods from Kate. I was sure she was delighted at the idea of a day without me moping around the house aimlessly.

"I don't see why not, son, as long as you promise to stay out of mischief," he said with a chuckle as if this could never be possible by the son of a Rear Admiral. "We leave the house at oh eight hundred sharp, so make sure you are ready to go."

"And, Thomas," Kate added, "perhaps you can wear one of those nice suits I had made for you. Not one of those Japanese things. You understand?"

So it was I had my first foray into an American big city. I felt quite dapper in my new navy blue suit and fedora. I quickly popped in and out of a couple of churches, just to ensure I had something to discuss over dinner, then wandered the streets, taking in the architecture, the vehicles and the white people who seemed to be everywhere I looked. Occasionally a black face would pass my line of vision, but they were always nannies pushing a white baby in a pram, or men stripped down to their shirtsleeves loading or unloading a truck. When at last I spotted a Chinese face I followed him at a discrete distance in the hope that he might lead me to a neighbourhood where I could find more Chinese, and maybe some Japanese people. It took a few tries, but eventually I found myself crossing Market Street and suddenly the signs on the shops were all in Chinese. That day I wandered up and down and in and out of every store, revelling in the familiar and marvelling at the trinkets that tourists were buying thinking they were 'Oriental'.

After my prompt and safe return that first day, with tales of the glory of the churches I had visited, there was never any questions asked. As long as I was dressed appropriately and waiting by the door at 'oh eight hundred hours', I was free to explore the city at will. I eventually tracked down a small community of Japanese immigrants called Nihonmachi. I could spend many hours sitting on the curb outside the Obayashi family's confectionary shop, especially later in the afternoon when the Japanese girls would be returning home from their jobs.

With the strange lack of seasonal changes, the weeks and months all rather blended together, but I remember one day, because it was the week after my father had decided somewhat arbitrarily, not knowing my actual birth date, that we would have a family dinner to celebrate my sixteenth birthday.

The following week, I was sitting at a sidewalk table outside a teahouse on Market Street, when I heard a voice from behind me.

"Excuse me. Could you perhaps tell me the time?"

It took me a moment to recognize that the voice was speaking Japanese and I turned to face the loveliest young woman I had ever seen. Her sweet smile vanished when she looked into my blue eyes.

"Oh, I am terribly sorry," she said in broken English. "I thought you Japanese."

"I am," I replied, feeling my heart expand with the sound of my native tongue. "Well, half-Japanese, half-American. That's why the eyes."

The smile returned and my expanded heart now started to do flips. "Would you perhaps join me for tea? I would very much like the company. Unless you have to be somewhere. I believe it is about three o'clock."

"Tea would be very nice, thank you," she said as she took the seat opposite me. "I am Marika. And you?"

"Thomas."

"Such an American name!" she laughed.

I stayed talking to Marika until I had to run in order to meet my father at the car for the ride home.

Every week after that, she and I would meet at the same spot. Sometimes we sat and talked. Sometimes she seemed enervated, with sparkling eyes and fidgety hands and we would walk the streets as we talked. She was fascinating and mercurial. She would never tell me where she lived or how she supported herself, though it was clear she was on her own. Her father had died in the same battle at Kwantung that had taken Fujio from me as a child. Her mother had remarried, to a man who, from what I could deduce, was very cruel to young Marika, so she had left as soon as she was able and met a man in Tokyo who arranged her passage to California. She had arrived with two other girls she had met on the boat, but the man had sent them up to San Francisco to work up there, while she was made to stay behind in San Diego. She told me that she too had been lonely since she had arrived, and how grateful she was that I had invited her to join me for tea that first day.

Suddenly it seemed that life in America wouldn't be so bad after all. The days I stayed at the house I hid in my room all day, writing embarrassingly sentimental love poems about Marika, and letters home to my aunt and uncle and to Robbie. Kate had happily convinced herself that I was seeking spiritual guidance each foray into the city, and I fed that belief by lustily declaring 'Amen' at the end of each supper's Grace and reading my bible passages with theatrical abandon. I rarely considered where the future would lead, but I was in love and content.

Then the day came. Marika and I were blissfully strolling arm in arm along 4th Avenue when I suddenly heard, "Thomas?"

I looked across the street and saw my father at the corner with two other navy officers. He briskly crossed to our side and stopped directly in front of me.

"What are you doing out here? And who is this… this… young woman?" he sputtered.

"Papa." I heard my voice quivering. "Papa, this is Marika. Marika, this is my father, Rear Admiral Pinkerton."

She looked at me with alarm in her eyes and I realized her problem.

"Rear Admiral is his title. Pinkerton is his name," I quickly explained in Japanese.

My father and Marika looked at each other. I was surprised to see my father's face go from beet red to ashen. When I glanced at Marika I saw a flash of defiance and what seemed to be a tiny smile lifted the corners of her lips.

"Son, I believe you should come back to the base with me and wait there till I am done work for the day."

"But, Marika…"

"I am sure that the young lady is perfectly capable of finding her own way back to wherever it is she lives."

With that, he turned and stepped off the curb again. I gave Marika a regretful look then took my place beside him for the quick march back to his office.

That night after the bible reading and the children had been sent off to bed, I received an endless lecture on how I had disappointed him, and how I had misled 'Mama'. He talked at length about the 'wrong type of girls', with Kate throwing in words like heathen and barbarian to make sure I got the point. Even as he was running out of ways to express his chagrin, I felt there was more he wanted to say, but he kept glancing over at Kate. In the end, he decreed that I was never to see the girl again and, with that, he opened his newspaper, she took up her needlepoint, and I was summarily dismissed.

For weeks I felt like a prisoner in that house. I became quite adept at avoiding Kate and Mr. Lawrence. In my mind I called him 'Loathsome Larry' as I knew instinctively that he was spying on my every move and reporting them to Papa at the end of each day. Mostly I hid in my room and wrote long romantic love poems to and about Marika. I figured out how to slip down to Papa's study unseen and most days by noon I was quite intoxicated on the whiskey I stole from his decanter. Finally one morning I couldn't stand it any longer.

After the usual breakfast gathering, where I stared down into my bowl of porridge and Benji and Lillian nattered on with endless questions about everything under the sun, Papa kissed Kate on the cheek, patted the children's heads, scowled at me and headed off to work. I faked a couple of coughs then informed Kate that I felt like I was coming down with a cold and was going to spend the day in bed. I was confident that she wouldn't check in on me. I locked my bedroom door, slipped out the window, carefully dropping to the soft grass below.

I knew it would take hours to walk the entire way into the city but was counting on the fact that most of the men in this neighbourhood worked downtown, so it wasn't long before a car loudly approached behind me. I raised my hand and the driver slowed to a stop.

"Excuse me sir," I addressed the gentleman seated in the back. "My father, perhaps you know him? Rear Admiral Pinkerton. I'm afraid we had a miscommunication today. He was supposed to drive me into the city today and he must have forgotten as he left without me. I don't suppose I could trouble you for a ride in?"

The man barely looked at me, just gave a brisk nod in the direction of the seat next to the driver and I gratefully climbed in.

Once I got to town I made haste to Market Street. I had no real plan. I realized that I had no idea where Marika lived or how I might find her, but I was determined that I would. I started at our usual teahouse. I asked the owner if he had seen her lately.

"She stopped in several times a few weeks ago. At first she took her tea and sat outside. It looked to me like she was waiting for you, young Master. Then for a while she would just walk in, look around, and walk out again. Now I'd say it's been at least two weeks since I saw her at all."

He could see my face fall. I had no idea, other than to rely on chance, how I could possibly find her.

"Perhaps," he began with hesitation in his voice, "perhaps you could head over to the Stingaree area. She might, perhaps, be found over there. You could ask the bartender at the saloon called The Old Tub of Blood if he has seen her."

I couldn't imagine that anyone at a saloon would know my sweet Marika, but I was willing to try anything, so I made my way over there. As I got deeper into the Stingaree it felt like some of the neighbourhoods in Tokyo that Robbie and I used to explore. Shabbily-dressed Chinese men squatted in doorways, smoking little cigarettes, the ground around them dotted with blobs of brown spit. Toothless old women watched heedlessly as filthy children threw pebbles at passing mule carts and wrestled on the dusty road. The occasional young woman would sashay past him, flashing him a beguiling smile as they passed.

Standing outside of the saloon, I took a deep breath and forced myself to stand tall. I swung open the door and was immediately hit with a cloud of stale beer and choking smoke. Through the haze I could see several men seated around tables, deeply engrossed in Fan-tan. Despite the early hour, they had all obviously been there gambling and drinking for several hours. When my eyes adjusted I made my way to the bar in the back where an old Chinese man was wiping glasses with a filthy rag. He looked up at me suspiciously.

The words rushed out of me. "I am looking for a young woman. Someone at the teahouse on Market suggested that you might know where I might find her. She is a girl named Marika. I'm afraid that is the only name I know."

For a few moments I thought perhaps he hadn't understood me. I had spoken to him in Cantonese and wondered if I was going to have to try again in my even worse Mandarin. He carefully placed the glasses back on the shelf behind him.

"Marika, you said? Sounds like a Japanese name to me. We don't have any Jap girls in here. You'll have better luck over at the Seven Buckets of Blood, or better still in Fifth and Island. That's where all the Japs live."

The Seven Buckets was nearby, so I headed there next. The same scenario greeted me. Even the bartender looked like he could have been the previous one's twin. I repeated my speech.

This time I saw a spark of recognition when he heard Marika's name. My heart skipped a beat.

"Marika? Sure, I know her. She wouldn't be in here until tonight, but I'm guessing you can probably find her over at Sam's place. You know where that is? No? Just head on over to J Street. About four buildings west of Sixth Avenue you'll see a red door. Just go on in there. She's probably there."

I practically ran the whole way there. The building was nondescript and the red door was unmarked. I thought I should knock, but the bartender had clearly said to walk in, so I pushed the door and stepped in.

The room was dark. Only a gas lamp sconce lit the space. The air was thick with an unfamiliar aroma and in the gloom I could see settees and cushions scattered around. Three Chinese men and one woman lounged around, all either cradling or drawing on long pipes. There was no sound but their heavy inhales. I couldn't imagine why my Marika would be here. I had heard about opium dens, but had, of course, never seen one. I was about to back out when a door in the back of the room opened. Light flooded in from the back alley and a female figure filled the doorway. The slim silhouette clearly showed a bustle-less skirt, a tight-fitted bodice and long hair flowing over her shoulders. The sunlight glared across the room, lighting me up while leaving her in darkness, and she froze in place.

"Thomas?" she whispered.

"Marika? Is that you?" Her shape seemed unfamiliar but the voice was unmistakable.

The door closed behind her and for a moment I could see nothing in the darkness, but I could hear her footsteps and the sweet aroma of lotus flower surrounded me.

Her voice was in my ear as she took my arm and leaned a little unsteadily on me. She spoke slowly. "Thomas, what are you doing here? Does your father know you are here? You shouldn't be here!"

I closed my eyes and breathed in her sweet scent. When I opened them again, I could see her more clearly. Her shiny black hair framed her heavily made-up face and trailed down to a low-cut bodice. Her breasts shone alabaster in the dim light. Her black eyes glittered.

"I have missed you so much, my darling. I couldn't stand it any longer! They can't prevent me from seeing you. I don't care what they say. Can we get out of here? Let's go for a walk, go have a tea. I have so much I want to say to you."

She took a step back from me and I watched her eyes try to focus on my face.

"I can't, Thomas. I need to stay here. My arrangement with Mr Lo, the owner is that I am here to help the clients during the day."

I looked around at the people in the room. None of them had moved since I had walked in, not even acknowledging my presence. The only movement was the slow, methodical transfer of the pipe from resting in their arms to raised to their lips.

"Can I just stay here with you, then? I need to talk to you. We need to plan how we can continue to see each other. You have missed me too, haven't you?"

"Thomas, of course I have. I looked for you the first few weeks after your father took you away, but I knew he would make it difficult for you to come back. Then I was needed here, and I was busy... elsewhere... and I guess I gave up hope of seeing you again."

Just then the door burst open and a tiny, ancient man marched in. He glared at me then addressed Marika.

"What are you doing? Is this young man a client? I have told you not to bring your business into my shop, Marika. You work your clients on your own time, not mine!"

"Oh no, Mr. Lo. This is a, um, new customer for you. I was just explaining the fees to him, then I will get him set up with a pipe. Isn't that right, sir?"

She looked at me desperately and I found myself nodding. She led me to a settee in a corner and took a pipe from a shelf.

"Please, Thomas, go along with this. I need Mr. Lo to allow me to stay. I can't afford to come here as a client and he lets me smoke as much as I want in exchange for being here for the others. Sit here. Have you tried opium before? Will you trust me? I know you will greatly enjoy the experience. It makes you feel so free and makes all the sorrow and anger go away. Just try it this once. It won't harm you and if you don't like it, well, I will never ask again."

So it was that I found myself lying on my side as she heated up the opium pill. I drew the smoke into my lungs and looked up at Marika expectantly. I had no idea what I would feel. It only took a few moments. Slowly a gentle calm settled in over me like a warm blanket. I felt all the anger that I had been bearing toward my father and Kate seem to wash away. My limbs felt heavy but the sensation gave me no concern. A small smile crossed Marika's lips as she watched me, then she stretched out on the cushions next to me. I took one more pull from the pipe then passed it down to her. I lost all track of time. We might have been lying there for a few minutes or a few hours. It didn't matter. I was content for the first time in my life.

The feeling didn't last long and when the anger and frustration returned, it seemed like I could no longer hold the emotions in check.

"Thomas, take me to the park to throw a ball," Benji demanded one day at breakfast.

Before I could stop myself, I slammed down my fork and yelled, "Don't talk to me like I am one of your damned servants, Benji! God! You are the most spoiled child I have ever met." And I got up to leave the table.

"Papa!" Benji whined.

"Thomas!" my father bellowed. "You will never speak to your brother like that again. You are the one who is a spoiled child and as long as you are under my roof, you will hold your tongue and not use that kind of language in front of the children or your mother."

"She's not my mother," I muttered.

"Your room. Now!"

I glared at him and smirked at Benji and stormed from the room.

The next day I slipped away, found a ride again, and made my way to the red door.

This became a pattern. I would manage to stay home and be relatively civil for a few days, then the anger would build up like a volcano in me and I would lash out. Once when Kate told me to take Lillian over to a neighbour's for a playdate, I crushed a crystal water glass in my hand and left a trail of bright red droplets of blood across the white carpet from the dining room to the kitchen sink

Marika and I didn't talk like we did when we first met, but I felt like I was growing more and more in love with her each time we lay together in that dark room. It was increasingly harder to tear myself away and meander my way back to the road home and occasionally a driver would have to nudge me awake when we reached our neighbourhood.

My seventeenth birthday came and went with little fanfare. Kate made a big deal over the fact that she had asked Cook to make my favourite food. Benji and Lilian had drawn birthday cards for me. Papa presented me with an expensive wristwatch. I did try my hardest to be cheerful and grateful but inside I was seething with rage and I had to clench my fists to hide my shaking hands. That night, after suffering through our nightly bible reading, I excused myself to my room and slipped out the window.

It took a long time before a car came along the road. I hadn't thought to bring a jacket and the night air was cool. By the time I climbed in beside the driver my teeth were chattering and I couldn't stop the shaking in my arms and legs.

"Bit of a chilly night to be out and about, son," the man said.

Perhaps he was just being conversational, but I was filled with the thought that he was distrustful and might report me to the authorities as a suspicious character lurking in the wealthy community. Through gritted teeth, I assured him that I was a resident and was just heading into the city to meet with friends.

"You're a little young to be out alone at this hour, aren't you?"

We were almost into the city at this point and when he stopped at a crossroad I threw open the door and bolted from the car. I ran all the way to the red door.

When I entered the room, just the smell in the air seemed to bring me some comfort. There were many men and a few women. All the settees were taken and the floor was filled with bodies. The only sound was the intake and exhale of smoke and the occasional rustle of fabric as someone changed to a more comfortable position. I waded through the room, looking at all the faces, searching for Marika but she wasn't there. Mr. Lo appeared from the back door and put out his one hand for money, as he held a pipe in the other.

"Mr. Lo, I, um, I didn't bring any money with me. Is Marika not here? Do you know where I might find her?"

He withdrew his hand and hesitated a moment, then offered me the pipe.

"I am sure you will be honourable and pay me double the next time, young man. Am I correct?"

My mind was still racing with thoughts of finding Marika, while my hand took over and reached for the pipe. I quickly found a spot on the floor, settled in and waited for the euphoria to come. I lost track of time again, until Mr. Lo crouched down on his heels beside me.

"I can tell you where to find Marika, if you like."

My eyes struggled to focus and with much effort I pulled myself up to sitting.

"Go two blocks west and one block south. There is a house there with a blue door and red curtains on the windows. You will find her there."

I stumbled down the street, mumbling to myself, "two blocks west, one block south, blue door, red curtains," over and over. I finally knew where my beloved lives! Maybe I could come live with her here. I could get out of that house and away from those hated people and be with my Marika for the rest of our lives.

I knocked on the door and waited. It seemed to be forever before the door opened a crack. The strong smell of incense struck me and a woman peered out at me.

"Yes?"

I was confused. This wasn't Marika. Maybe it was her mother? I self-consciously tugged at my collar and ran a hand through my hair.

"I am looking for Marika. Is she here? My name is Thomas. Perhaps she has mentioned me?"

The woman laughed, her bright red lips parting to show criss-crossed teeth.

"No, young man. She hasn't mentioned you. But you are welcome to come in. Marika is occupied right now, but she should be available soon if you wish to wait."

She opened the door wider and ushered me into a small room. The couple of oil lamps had red glass which cast an eerie glow. She signalled for me to sit on a couch against one wall. When I did, I realized that there was a young Japanese woman, a girl really, sitting in an overstuffed armchair opposite me. She had one leg tucked under her and the silky drape of her skirt exposed her other leg to her knee. Her bodice was slightly undone as well and her hair was hanging loose around her shoulders. Her head was tilted slightly and her eyes were unfocused as if she had just woken from a long sleep. She was lazily smoking a tiny cigarette held delicately between her thumb and finger.

"Hello honey. You here for some company?" she asked me in English with a thick accent.

Just then an older American man in a naval uniform came down the stairs, straightening his tie as he did. He glanced at me and smirked.

"Hey, kid. You're a little young, aren't you? Ah hell. Have fun." And he let himself out the front door.

The girl across from me seemed to have forgotten I was there and was intently picking at some dirt under her long fingernails. I was just about to go off in search of Marika when she came down the stairs and into the room. She was wrapped in a silk robe. Her bare toes with bright red polish peeked out from the hem. She had the same tousled hair and slightly glazed eyes as the armchair girl.

"Thomas? What are you...? How did you find...? My darling, I have missed you!" She ran to me and kissed me. Now we had kissed before, but never like this. Her kiss sent shock waves straight to my penis. Embarrassed by my obvious physical reaction, I held her slightly away from me but she sidled out of my grasp and slipped in close and pressed her hip into my aching crotch.

Her eyes glittered up at me as she whispered, "Shh, come upstairs, quickly. Aino-san doesn't like it when we have guests."

I would like to say that the first time was magical, but it certainly wasn't. I managed to get my boots and pants off, all the while staring at Marika as she lay on her bed in that maidenly flimsy robe, then proceeded to ejaculate in my union suit. She patiently took my hand and guided me to lie beside her. The ever-present opium pipe was by her side and she lit it, took a draw and passed it to me. The opium's immediate effect took hold and I felt totally at peace. It wasn't long before I was ready to try again and this time we had some success, although I am sure she felt no satisfaction. We lay there through the night, smoking and making love and talking.

"Thomas, I am starting to feel like San Diego isn't the right place for me. I have been thinking that maybe I should go to Japan. See if I can find my family there."

"Marika! You can't leave me!"

"Maybe I will could go ahead and check it out. We would only be apart for a few months at most, then I will write and tell you if it is where I want to stay. Then we could plan how you could come over too."

My befuddled mind tried to grasp what she was saying.

"I would move there with you? Yes... Yes, I could get a job. We could live together. We could get married and have children and..."

"Slow down, Thomas. Let's take it one step at a time. In a few weeks, when I have enough money, I will find a ship to take me there."

The next few weeks I took crazy risks, sneaking out of the house late at night to be with Marika as often as possible before she left. Papa's car was parked in the drive shed in the back. He had let the driver go, and was driving himself now, so there was no one in the apartment above the shed to hear when I figured out how to start the car and, with much hiccuping and stalling, learned to drive it well enough to get down to the house with the red curtains. I also had to slip into Papa's study during the day, without being seen. I had seen him take cash from an envelope in his desk drawer when Kate wanted to go dress shopping. And Marika insisted that, if she spent the night with me, she wasn't working and Aina-san expected her rent. So I would always leave her some of the pilfered cash when I slipped out before dawn.

I guess I had sort of figured out that she was a call-girl but I loved her so much that I convinced myself that this was just what she had to do to survive, being all alone in the world. Once she and I were married, of course, I would support her and she would never have to do that again. Somehow, in my opium-fogged brain, that all made perfect sense.

It was in the third week of our affair that everything came crashing down. It was about two in the morning and we were wrapped in each other's arms, dozing off for a bit before she could entice me to hardness and we could make love again. She had been a great teacher and I was amazed at all the sublime ways and means of sex.

Suddenly the door flew open and there stood my father. Even in the soft light of a single lamp I could see the rage glittering in his eyes.

"How did you find me?" I stammered.

"Lillian was fussing, so Kate went into her room to check on her. She happened to glance out the window back there and noticed that the car was missing."

Before he could continue, Marika's groggy voice rose up from the bed beside me.

"And he knew to come here because he used to come to see me here," she said. "His wife was pregnant, so he would come here for the sex he wasn't getting at home. He told me I reminded him of a young prostitute he bedded whenever he went to Japan. He even insisted on calling me Butterfly."

I looked down at her. She lay defiantly naked in the bed, her tiny breasts glowing pale in the half-light.

"I am sorry, Thomas. I recognized him when we ran into him on the street that day but I didn't know how to tell you. It would have meant explaining how I... make my living, and I was afraid you would leave me if you knew."

My mother, I thought. He called my mother a prostitute. Auntie Su had told me about my mother, about how she had trained and was one of the most sought-after geishas in Nagasaki. How being a geisha was considered an honourable profession, one that required great skill as a singer, musician, hostess, and not shameful at all. How my father had won her hand over that of a prince because he loved her that much. Suddenly I understood everything. He hadn't loved her. He had just toyed with her affection for his own pleasure. And she had killed herself when she realized she would never have his love. He had basically killed her himself. As I turned my gaze to him, standing silently in the doorway, his rage seemed to shift to humiliation and I saw him as a pathetic, loathsome man.

I went back to the house with him that night. We were completely silent all the way and I went straight to my room. I stayed there until I knew he had gone off to work in the morning. When I did finally open my door, Benji raced up the stairs, full of the morning's exciting news.

"Thomas! Did you hear? Someone came in the night and stole Papa's car! He hired a driver and went out to find it and when he did, he managed to convince the hooligan to give it back. He's so brave! Can you imagine? The car is back and safe again and Papa has told Mama not to worry, that the young man has learned his lesson and won't be coming around to try that nonsense again. I sure wish I had woken up to see Papa when he came home! You don't mess around with Rear Admiral Pinkerton, that's for sure!"

I murmured some vague words of agreement which seemed to satisfy the boy as he turned and raced off to share the news of his father's exploits with his nanny.

A few days later, when I knew the coast was clear, I slipped out of my room in search of a morning coffee. An envelope lay on the floor outside my door. It was addressed to me in Uncle Bart's chicken-scratch handwriting. The sight of it made me smile as I padded barefoot into the kitchen and poured myself the lukewarm dregs from my father's breakfast coffee pot. The house was silent, so I took my cup into Kate's sunroom and perched on a settee to read the letter.

"August 14, 1923 My dear Thomas, I have received some disturbing news from your father. He has expressed concern that you are not settling in as well there as we had hoped. He says you have been acting out and suspects you might be taking opium. This has your Auntie Su and I both gravely concerned. As I hope you know, we love you as if you were our son and it tears us apart to think of you struggling so, with us so far away. So we have made a decision. I am resigning my post here at the embassy and have accepted a position teaching at Stanford University. I had hoped to find a professorship in San Diego or Los Angeles but San Francisco is not that far away. We would like you to come up there as soon as we are settled in. I have a great deal to do here before we can leave, and of course Auntie Su won't go until after the cherry blossoms have fallen! By the time we get everything packed up and make the crossing, I anticipate we will be arriving in San Francisco by the end of September. I know that seems like a long time from now, but please do your best to behave as the respectful young man your Aunt and I raised you to be and we will see you soon. Affectionately, your Uncle Bart. PS I understand there is also some issue with a young lady. We can discuss that as well, since, as you know, I have some experience with falling in love with a Japanese girl...."

    Father came home early that day. He called me into his study. He was sitting behind his desk and I was surprised to see Kate there, ram-rod straight on a chair to his left, her Bible on her lap and clutching a hankie which she occasionally dabbed non-existent tears from her eyes. I stood in front of the desk, ready for yet another lecture.
    "Thomas, my boy, I'm afraid I have sad news. I received a telegraph this afternoon. There was a massive earthquake in Japan yesterday. Most of Tokyo was levelled. Your friend Robbie (last name?) and his family didn't survive."
    "But Auntie Su and Uncle Bart did, right? They were already onboard their ship heading to San Francisco, right?"
    I heard Kate let out a little whimper.
    "Son, I am sorry. Their ship was scheduled to depart today. Authorities have already identified their bodies among those pulled from the rubble of the American embassy."
    I stared blankly at him, unable to absorb this news. Kate's high sing-song voice cut through the fog.
    "You know, God's people, the missionaries over there, have been warning the Japanese for years to give up their barbaric beliefs. There are prophecies, you know..." She opened her Bible and started leafing

through as though she could find just the right passage to defend her theory.

"Kate. Not now, please," Papa said curtly.

Her cheeks reddened and she carefully closed the book on her lap, glaring at me as if all of this was somehow my fault. I stared blankly at the two people sitting in front of me. They seemed to be strangers to me. Then I somehow managed to make my legs work and I stiffly left the room. I absently noticed the children hovering just outside the door, their eyes as wide as saucers as I brushed past them.

I found myself in the entryway. My body ached to grab the doorknob and run, run to town, run to Marika, run to opium and the cure for this pain and anger that was building in my gut. I turned slowly in the big open space and my eyes settled on the ever-present vase of lilies. For the first time I realized that the pattern winding around the crimson vessel was a spiral of cherry blossom boughs interwoven with butterflies in flight. Then I remembered something Kate had told me shortly after I had first arrived at the house. She was overseeing as Mr. Lawrence did the weekly chore of replacing the lilies with new, fresh ones.

"I love this vase, Thomas. In fact, I think this might be my favourite thing in the whole house! It was my wedding gift from your father. Such a thoughtful man! Isn't it beautiful?"

The memory and the idea that he had given her something so Japanese, so much an obvious reminder to him of my mother, made me snap. I don't remember picking up the vase and hurling it at the door, but I heard the crash and saw the white marble floor littered with tiny shards of deep red ceramic. It looked like a million drops of blood scattered through the entryway.

I stormed to my room and slammed and locked the door. In a few moments I heard Papa's voice speaking sharply out in the hallway.

"Son, I know this news has upset you, but you cannot act out like that in this house. I am going to work and I suggest you spend the day in there, thinking about your actions. We will talk when I get home."

When twilight darkened my room and I hadn't heard any sounds out in the hallway, hunger finally got the better of me and I slipped out in search of food. There was a note in my father's handwriting lying on the floor outside my door. I grabbed it and headed down the stairs, my bare feet silent in the thick carpet. I crossed the entryway, glancing at the table which now sat bare without its constant companion. There was a single light on in the kitchen. I took an apple from the bowl on the counter, took a bite and read the note.

"Thomas, I understand that moving here has been an adjustment for you. Your mother and I have tried to be patient and give you time to settle in. But your behaviour has become more and more trying and shows no sign of improvement. Your actions this morning was the last straw. You upset your mother so much that she now fears for her safety and the safety of her children. When I came home today, I discovered that she has taken Benji and Lilian and gone to stay at her parents' home until this situation is resolved. Butterfly once told me that she used to call you "Sorrow" and I am now beginning to realize that that is in fact what you have brought into this house.

"I am too angry and distraught to discuss what the next action must be. I have retired to my room for the night. I suggest you give some serious thought to taking on a job so you can move out of this house as soon as possible. Father"

My mind was spinning. Too many emotions overcame me. My father and Marika. Uncle Bart and Auntie Su. And now this. How could I find a job? Where would I live? I stood frozen, the note in one hand and a half-eaten apple in the other. I forced myself to take deep breaths. Marika! The answer lay with Marika. I could convince Marika to leave with me.

Maybe we could go up to San Francisco together. I could find a job on the docks. We could get married, find a little home of our own up there. We could leave all this sorrow behind us.

With a plan in place, I raced up and got my shoes and threw a few things into a bag. Slipping out the door, I ran to the road and flagged down the first car heading down to town. From there I ran through the dimly lit streets until I arrived at the house with the red curtains. By the time I knocked on that familiar door, a sense of resolve had flowed into me. I could feel the blood coursing through my body as I knocked. Aina-san opened the door.

"I need to see Marika!" I practically shouted at the tiny woman.

She scowled at me and her heavily-made-up eyes glittered in the darkness.

"You! You want to see Marika? Well, good luck with that! I should have you beaten and tossed to the curb. Marika was my best girl here, and now she is gone."

"Gone? But where? Why did she go?"

"She informed me yesterday that she is pregnant, that's why. What use is a pregnant call-girl to me? This isn't a home for wayward girls. It is a business. What? I am going to have some squalling brat under my roof? I sent her packing."

"But please tell me. Where did she go?"

"She went over to the Naval base and paid a visit to that big shot officer that used to be her customer. You know him - the one that barged into the house a few days ago. She came back and told me that he had given her a good sum of money as long as she left right away. Who knows? Maybe the child is his. Or yours?"

She let out an ugly grunt of a laugh.

"Then she packed her things and got a ticket for the ship leaving this morning for Japan. Said she was going to go back to her family and see if they would take her back. Not that they are likely to want an opium-addicted, used-up prostitute and her bastard child. But good riddance, I say. Now, unless you are interested in the services of one of my other lovely young ladies, I suggest you get off my stoop."

She waited a moment for my response. When I just stood staring at her, she shrugged her shoulders and closed the door in my face.

Opium, I thought. I need opium. Opium will help me figure out what to do. Opium will help me think straight. I sprinted the few blocks to the house with the red door. For a moment I stood, leaning against the door frame, my lungs heaving and my entire body shaking, then I threw open the door and found myself standing in a cold, dark, empty room. Gone were all the cushions and settees. The shelves that lined the walls that had just recently held all the pipes not sat barren. I shook my head, wondering what kind of nightmare I had found myself in. Remembering that Mr. Lo had a private room at the back, I fumbled around in the blackness until I found the hidden door and banged loudly on it. In a few moments the door opened a crack and I could just make out the old man's face.

"Mr. Lo! What's happened? Where is everyone?"

He shook his head sadly.

"All gone. The coppers raided my shop yesterday. I was here in back. They arrested my customers and the boy who was helping me. They took everything away as evidence. Seized all my dope too. They didn't find me. I hid here in back. I am packing up and getting away before they know this is my shop and come back to find me. Luckily your girl, Marika, wasn't here. She was here the day before, but I haven't seen her since then. You tell her when you see her, okay? Tell her Mr. Lo is out of business so she will need to hit the pipe somewhere else."

He disappeared back behind the door again. I don't remember leaving the shop but my feet automatically headed back to the road home. Everything was lost. I didn't want to go back to that house, but I had nowhere else to go, and no-one to turn to. Everything had seemed so perfect and now it was all gone. A driver with a horse-drawn cart offered me a lift. I mumbled where I was going, then climbed into the back of the cart and curled up in a ball next to the crates he was delivering.

When I got home, everything was as silent as when I had left. I momentarily wondered where Mr. Lawrence and the cook were, but it didn't matter to me and I didn't care. Down the hall off the entryway I could see a dim light coming from Papa's study and realized that he was in there, probably drinking his scotch, smoking a cigar, and reading his paper. Like nothing had happened. Like the entire world hadn't come crashing in on itself. I felt utterly exhausted and deflated. I dragged myself up the stairs and closed the door of my room behind me.

I sat on my bed for a long time. I had no sense of time but the room had grown completely dark. Then slowly the moon began to rise and shone its bright beam through my open window and across the room. A glint caught my eye. I realized that the moonlight was shining directly on the object on my dresser. My Mama-san's tanto knife rested in its stand. I had always known the story of this knife. I knew about my grandfather's seppuku and my mother's suicide. The knife should have been a hated thing, something long ago discarded. But it had been the only legacy I had brought from Japan. It always felt, as macabre as it seemed, to be a link to my history.

The knife was in my hands. Some deeply buried memory from my early childhood surfaced and I knelt on the floor as I had seen Mama-san kneeling as I peered around Uncle Bart's legs. By then her body had been doubled over onto itself, wrapped in her wedding kimono, surrounded by a widening circle of blood. But I knew how she had knelt to perform the act. With my face to the moon, I held up the blade so it shone fiercely in the white light. My mind was blank. All I knew was a deep desire for peace. With all my strength I thrust the knife upward into my gut. The pain was excruciating but at the same time I felt gratitude for it. I let out a low grunt but didn't cry out. I watched in awe as the blood flowed from my body, quickly soaking into the white carpet below me. It was like I was kneeling on a pink cloud. I pulled the knife back out and, with my last remaining strength, I wiped the blood off the blade, using a corner of the white bedspread and placed the knife carefully beside me. Light-headed I had a momentary thought.

"Oh Kate is going to be so angry when she sees how I have stained the bedding."

Then I slumped over and lay on my side on the damp, sticky carpet. I had no more thoughts. I felt nothing but the peace I had so longed for. My eyes were closed and I lay breathing in the sharp, metallic smell. I was just about to let myself drift away when far off in the distance I heard a knocking on my door and the rattle of my doorknob. Then my father's voice, tinged in fear, like an echo of a long-ago time.

"Thomas! Thomas!"

Made in the USA
Lexington, KY
23 August 2019